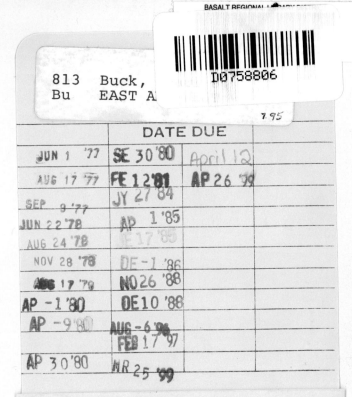

East and West

East and West

STORIES BY

Pearl S. Buck

THE JOHN DAY COMPANY
New York

Designed by Ingrid Beckman

Manufactured in the United States of America

Library of Congress Cataloging in Publication Data

Buck, Pearl Sydenstricker, 1892-1973.
    East and West.

    CONTENTS: Until tomorrow.—Fool's sacrifice.—
The golden bowl. [etc.]
    I. Title.
PZ3.B8555Ear4   [PS3503.U198]   813'.5'2
ISBN 0-381-90015-0   75-11609

10 9 8 7 6 5 4 3 2 1

Contents

Until Tomorrow

CHINA—1930s

THE WHITE WOMAN LAY stretched straight in her bed in the late afternoon of the hot July day, listlessly watching the Chinese woman as she tucked in the edges of the mosquito net about her. She was eager to be alone in the dimness of the sheltered room, eager for the other woman to hasten herself and be gone, but in spite of her eagerness she could not avoid a wave of tenderness as she looked at the small, stooping, blue-coated figure, searching meticulously for an aperture through which a mosquito might crawl and disturb her mistress. In the background of the white woman's alien, lonely life in this foreign country, there was always this little dark figure, scarcely noticed, stooping over a tub, bending over sewing, rising and trotting to answer a bell, slipping into her room to announce a meal. How much of her comfort, the white woman thought with compunction, belonged to this Chinese woman, and yet how little she really knew or thought about her even after all these years.

She was moved to ask suddenly, "Amah, you have children?"

The answer came like a sigh. "No, my mistress, they are all dead."

"But you have a husband?"

"Yes," the woman answered quietly. Then she left the bed and peered into the thermos carafe on the table. It was evidently not full. "That lazy Wang Li," she muttered. "He never keeps this full."

She left the room an instant and returned, the bottle securely corked to keep the water fresh and iced. Then she stood looking about the room. Anne Page watched her, knowing she would not go until all was as she wished. She straightened the brushes upon the dressing table, picked up a pair of silken hose, shut a closet securely. Then, her hand upon the door, she said softly, "Until evening, my mistress."

"Until evening," replied Anne Page, wearily.

So at last she was left alone in the darkness. She had been looking forward all day to this hour of lonely darkness. All the time she had been packing Henry's food box for his journey of inspection into the interior stations, where his firm was growing tobacco among the Chinese farmers, she had looked forward to this hour. She had borne Henry's loud distractions, his anxieties over the box and the bedding, his little multitude of worries, his fussiness, she called it secretly, to which she could scarcely become accustomed even after all these years. But through the day she had said to herself, "I can bear it because the night is coming, and I shall be alone in the house. Rodney will come this evening. I shall be able to talk with him again and he to me. And I shall be alone all night and until day after tomorrow. So I can bear this day."

And she had borne it. She had held her soft smile fixed as she went swiftly here and there, giving this command and that to the flying servants, herself inspecting the tinned meats and vegetables going into the food box to make sure nothing was put in that Henry did not like, herself counting his linen suits and herself rolling up the thin woven mat upon which he slept instead of a sheet for coolness in the heat of summer. This smile she kept while he kissed her, and when he shouted, "Well, Anne, old girl, it'll be a long two days for me without you, I can tell you!" she had answered, "And for me, too,

Henry, my dear." She had returned his kiss gently—how many years had it been since she had kissed him with passion? —had left her hand quiet in his grasp while they walked to the gate of the compound together, and she had stood there in the afternoon sun while he swung himself upon his horse.

"Well, so long, Anne," he shouted, looking at her affectionately. "God, I never get used to leaving home, Anne," he added.

"Goodbye, dear. I think you have everything. It's only two days," she answered mildly.

A little crowd of passersby and street children had gathered instantly, and forgetting her, he cried excitedly at them, in broken Chinese, "Get out—get out—the horse comes!"

The crowd shrank back, and Anne closed the door quickly. She could never bear that loud voice of his shouting at the people without being somehow ashamed for him. They were not people to him, and to her everyone was a person. Each little brown child she passed on the street and smiled at was a little person in his own right. "Sentimental," Henry said to her stoutly, and then, with large, tolerant affection, "But it's all right for you to be any way you like. It's all right with me, old girl, however you are."

Oh, she thought wearily in the darkness, there was no doubt that Henry loved her. His ardent, boisterous love, she thought, was the hardest thing she had to bear. "I wonder," she thought to herself in the darkness, smiling a little bitterly, "if there is any other woman of thirty-seven in the world who complains even to herself because her husband still loves her after they have been married thirteen years!" Had she ever loved him? How could she know now?

Well, then, after the gate was shut she had turned into her garden. Suddenly, with Henry gone, it was a place of beauty and peace. Strange how when he was in it she saw nothing of it. It seemed all filled with noise and with his great burly presence. Now when he was gone, the flowers became delicately themselves once more. A mimosa that had been shivering grew still. A red monthly blooming rose glowed out intensely from the vine-covered wall. The grass grew green again, the shadows under the bamboos were marked and deeply cool. A bird sang. She drew a soft breath and felt her whole body relax into the beauty. Now she could rest. She could turn her thoughts away from Henry for two whole days. The gate had closed after him. She would eat an early dinner, go upstairs and undress and lie upon the mat on her bed and prepare for this other life of hers, this deep sweet secret life that was beginning to pour in on her, this friendship, this life with Rodney.

But even while she was thinking of him, she had slept, exhausted, and when she woke it was twilight, and the Chinese woman had come in and touched her gently on the hand and said, "The tall Englishman awaits my mistress."

Rodney—already! To what hour had she slept? She leaped up glancing at her little clock. It was a quarter to eight, and she had told him to come at eight!

There was no time to think of anything then except to brush her hair quickly and slip into the blue chiffon he liked. But she felt fresh and suddenly very happy as she went down the stairs. The house was so unaccustomedly quiet and full of repose. Wang Li had put flowers on the Chinese hall table, a bowl of the red roses, and they were reflected by the candlelight upon the dark polished wood. The hall door stood open to the garden and a soft fragrant darkness streamed into the house. She and Rodney—she and Rodney—alone in this quiet house! A sudden sense of well-being filled her heart.

But she went into the long drawing room quietly in her graceful, rather sedate fashion, her eyes searching the candlelit dimness for his slender form. He stood by an open French window, looking out into the darkness of the veranda beyond it, his back to her.

"Rodney," she said, quietly.

"Anne," he replied as quietly, but he did not turn. Her heart began to beat quickly. She went up to him and put out her hand to touch him and then waited, puzzled and a little afraid. Every other time he had turned to her swiftly. This time he did not turn. He drew hard on his cigarette and stood, staring into the dark garden, unresponding to her touch.

"Rodney," she said, her whole voice an anxious question, "have I hurt you somehow, without knowing it?"

He waited a moment and then replied, his voice pleasant, modulated, but strangely determined, "No, Anne—except—unless—one could say you hurt me by being what you are—always kind and good to everybody—and especially to Henry and to me alike." He paused. She took her hand from his sleeve and put it to her lips and waited, astounded, for his next word. He continued, staring into the darkness, "I've come to the crossroads, Anne, this week while I've been waiting for tonight. I can't go on this way—not any longer. Here I am, a man of forty-three, and here you are a woman of thirty-seven. We are not young any more. We haven't many more years. Henry is forty, and the halest of the three of us. He will outwear both you and me. We know that. And anyway we are not the sort, you and I—to count on anything—unforeseen—happening. That would be revolting. I can't. I've got to take the direct way. I've got to come out into the open now, and tell him what you are to me, that you are the only woman I've ever known whom I want to marry, and that you love me. I know it will be hard on him—he'll mind it damnably at first. But he won't mind as much as I will with-

out you. He is that jolly sort—he'll find someone else probably. You know—"

He stopped and began his furious smoking again. She sat
down quietly in the dim room and in the dimness leaned back
against the chair and closed her eyes and turned her head
away. So they must go into all this, she thought wearily.
Once before Rodney was swept by this mood of impatience,
and firmly and quietly she had held him as her friend, not
her lover. But she could not bear it tonight. It would mean a
long evening of agonizing argument, the more agonizing because between them both would hang the knowledge of their
love, their passionate, intimate love, that neither could do
without and yet that was sorrow to them both; to her, sorrow because she never could be with Rodney without seeming to see Henry's hurt boyish face beside her, and to
Rodney, sorrow because he knew she saw that face, and in
his delicacy shrank from that knowledge and then pressed
against it, seizing her the more ardently, demanding the more
of her until she was faint with his ardor. And all the time
they knew—oh, by now they both knew—that secret love was
never happy. Love needed the sunshine and the open, like a
flower, and struggled toward it always—that is, if it were real
love, as theirs was.

"Rodney," she said unsteadily without opening her eyes,
"tonight I am so weak—if you press me too much tonight—"
Her lips trembled and she stopped. He turned quickly and
dropped to his knees before her and buried his face in her
lap. Then he searched and found her hands and held them
to his face, and his cheeks burned against her palms. They
stayed silent and she could feel his passion begin to mount.
He did not move, nor did she move, but passion began to
fuse them together. Her heart beat hard and suddenly. She
was afraid. Tonight—would she be able to withstand him to-

night—did she wish to withstand him? At this moment she could not see Henry at all. She thought of him desperately, tried to remember what he looked like this afternoon. She could see his great burly body, even hear his big voice; but his face was blank. She could only feel Rodney's face here between her hands, his thin, hard cheeks, brown and hard.

"Rodney—" she began, her voice faint and far away in her own ears.

But the door opened suddenly. Rodney leaped to his feet. A small stooping Chinese woman stood in the doorway, framed against the light. "Mistress," she said tonelessly, "what time do you bathe yourself this night so that I may have the water ready?"

A great revulsion swept through Anne Page's body. Something—this little figure—had cut the passion between her and the man. She could not have said whether she were glad or sorry. She answered, "I think at eleven, Amah."

The woman hesitated, motionless in the doorway. "And shall I put on the light in this room, mistress?" she asked. "Is it not better to have more light now that the night is come?"

Out of the darkness Anne rose quickly and herself went to a lamp. "I was about to do so, Amah," she answered evenly. A touch and the room was full of light. Rodney was standing by the window again looking out into the dark garden. The Chinese woman looked at him once, quickly, and went away, leaving the door open into the hall.

The two stood silent a moment, Anne by the light, Rodney looking into the garden. Both of them were too proud to confess to each other their dread of servants' talk, of being discovered by servants. It was a desecration to have their love become servants' talk. They were even now embarrassed.

Then suddenly Rodney went to the door and closed it.

"Let's have this out, Anne," he said. "I'll sit here. You sit here. I won't touch you. See, like this. This is mind working with mind now—no bodies to interfere with reason."

He waited for her to sit in the wicker chair under the light and then he seated himself not too near her. The light fell soft and full upon her brown hair and upon the dull blue dress. But he cast only a quick glance at her and then looked away and began to speak evenly and coolly.

"I'll put the case, Anne," he said, staring down at the cigarette he held in his fingers.

"Here are Henry and I, both loving you. I'll be as fair as I can to Henry. We are not friends, as you know. Not enemies either—only men too different to be friends. But I've never needed friends. I've been solitary, independent all my life. Whatever there has been in my life you know—once or twice a love affair—not love. This is not the same. I'll not get over you. We both know that. I want to marry you, and I've never wanted to marry before, knocking about the East as I have. Not, anyway, I think. I haven't the urge for children some men have, nor for home. I'd have said until two years ago when you and I first—loved each other—that I would never have wanted a woman permanently. I've waited these two years to get over you. And I know I cannot. I don't know why. I've seen women more beautiful by far than you are—younger. I shan't talk the usual stuff lovers talk. The fact remains I cannot get over you. I want you and none other. Young or old, beautiful or not, I don't care. I want you always. There I am, Anne. As for externals, you know me. Forty-three, tired a good deal of the time, frightfully keen on books and solitary things, no good at golf and the club and dancing and the other things men do here in this rotten river port. But I shan't go home. I like this country, I like the people—I like delving into this life in my solitary fashion. I'll stay here the rest of my life, I know. Once I thought I'd write. Now I know I'll never do anything except work enough to hold my job and live as I always have. Only we couldn't stay here. I'd apply to the office for a post in some other port. But you know me—you know my life. If you come to me I'll promise you only one thing—you shall have unfailing and tender understanding."

His voice shook. But he went on after a moment. "If I have to give you proof, then I dare to ask you to remember that night, now nearly three years ago, when your baby died. I don't fear to be unfair to Henry when I ask you to remember that you knew the little child was very ill and you sent for Henry—and I saw what you put in that piteous note —and he was in the club playing poker and he sent back word he'd be along as soon as the game was over. He thought you —overnervous—about the child. Anne, if you had sent me a message like that, do you think anything on this earth would have kept me away from you an instant? Do you think, if the child had been ours, that I would not have been by you every hour?"

Anne put up her hand defensively. Why did she feel always she must defend Henry? Perhaps because he was so inarticulate himself, so clumsy at saying things, that when Rodney's incisive speech dealt with him she defended him as she might a child. "Rodney—he—the baby was all right at three o'clock when Henry went to the club. It was so quick. You know Henry hasn't much imagination. He couldn't see how it could be so quick."

"So you have said when we talked of this before," said Rodney. Still he did not look at her. At last he went on. "Let it be so. But remember that it was I, then almost a stranger, here by chance, who stayed by you. I wanted to go and fetch Henry—do you remember? But the doctor said—he said there would not be time—and you said, 'Stay with me. I am so alone.' "

"Yes," said Anne faintly. "I know I said that." She looked down at her hands clasped upon her lap. Staring at them she could see again that little beloved body, her two-year-old only child, the only child she had ever had, wasted by cholera, dying. It was Rodney who had been beside her then, Rodney who had stood waiting when she had thrown herself beside the bed and clasped the child to her, Rodney who when the last quiver had passed over the little face, had unloosed her arms and led her away into the other room and then with that shy delicate way that was his he had received her into his arms and let her weep against him. It had been the first time in her life since she was a little child that she had wept against another. It had been sweet even then. Even then she had thought with wild relief that Henry was not there and so for a moment she could weep and be cared for, though by a stranger. If Henry had been there he would have been half insane with his own grief and she would have had to turn herself from her dead child to comfort him; as indeed, she had been compelled to do many times, and even now, sometimes, when he thought, rarely, of little Harry. What a rest and a fortification it had been to remember that first moment when she had, without thought of anyone except herself, her own grief, leaned against Rodney and been cared for.

"In that moment," said Rodney quietly, his long body motionless, his long delicate hands crossed upon his knees now, "in that moment our love was born. I knew it, and later you told me you knew it. No wonder, then, that it does not die."

There was a long silence between them. Neither made a move toward the other. At last Rodney began to speak again. "So much I say for myself. I could tell you again the story of our love these two years, how long we both knew it and how we would not speak; how suddenly I did speak that Christmas eve, the first after Harry died. I came in here, knowing how hard that eve would be for you, fearing lest I intrude upon you and your husband, and yet fearing even more that you might be alone. You were alone. He had gone somewhere to play bridge and you—"

Again she had that swift impulse of defense for Henry. "I had told him I had a bad headache. It was not his fault, really. He would have stayed if I had asked him."

"But you felt it easier for you to have him gone. You were less lonely with your sorrow when he was gone," Rodney finished for her.

She could not deny it. Her head sank lower.

"On that evening, when I came in, when I saw you lying on that long chair before the fire, I went straight to you and said, 'I love you.' You might have repulsed me. I thought, as soon as the words were out of my lips, that you would. You are not the sort of woman who would welcome a love affair. Nor did I want a love affair with you. I did not even think of that term in connection with you. I simply loved you, and suddenly had to have you know it. It was nearly six months before you told me you loved me and said that could be all. But I would have waited forever—or gone forever without hearing those words and waited—O my love!"

Passion leaped out of his voice again. He threw her his quick warm look, subdued himself, and then went on in the same quiet voice. "What has happened since we both know. It is not necessary for me to tell it, since we have lived it together. All that I shall say is that now I have come to a place where I must have a decision from you. I cannot go on as we have been doing. This is no hole-and-corner affair. We are not common people, seeking a little excitement and variety as

common people will. This is you and I, and our whole remaining life. Will you have me, Anne? If you will, then we
must come out into the open and come together rightly."

He waited, but still she made no answer. At last he spoke
again. "So much for me. Now for Henry. Henry married
you when you were both young. You told me yourself that
you were not sure you loved him, even then—that you had
been boy and girl together in a small American town, that he
got this post in China, and wrote back to you, asking you to
come. It was romantic—Henry was in love with you—"

"He is still in love with me—" she said in a low voice.

"Oh, I know, as he understands love. He has used you, demanded everything of you as though he were your child instead of your husband upon whom you ought to be able to
lean. You've made his life easy—made this home—your creation. But I will be fair to him. Let's say he loves you the best
he can. But he's never—valued you."

He was staring at her, his eyes black under his heavy
brows. Now he was smoking his pipe. She saw his hand
curved about the bowl and was stung by an instant's passion
for it. She loved that thin hand of his, seeing it beautiful always in its contrast to Henry's thick hands. But she did not
answer.

"Of course," said Rodney dispassionately, "Henry is a
very decent fellow. When he goes into the club, everybody
shouts at him and wants to drink with him. I'll grant he is as
good to you as he knows how to be. He'd probably be very
much upset if I, for instance, should tell him he had absorbed
you selfishly"—his voice suddenly changed—"and to what
end, my darling, my darling? Oh, Anne, if he had been a
great man of some sort, if all the absorption of you had gone
into making him bigger and finer, I wouldn't say a word now.
But he absorbs you, he demands everything of you, all your

delicacy and your talent and your grace and everything that is you is sucked into him and lost. He is not finer, not more sensitive, no more worthy than if none of you had gone into him. Any woman might have done for him—not you—not you—oh my God, the waste!"

He rose from his chair and rushed to her, and kneeling, he seized her in his arms. "Oh Anne, Anne," he said brokenly, his head pressed into her shoulder.

She held herself outwardly rigid. She dared not move within his arms lest she yield finally. But within herself the movement she knew so well began, the melting of the heart, the rush of the blood, the great flowing out of love toward him. Oh, she wished she could be alone first, outside the circle of these arms, that she might know what she ought to do —what she really wanted to do! How could she decide now, like this—

She began to tremble and to look here and there about the room, yet seeing only this dark head.

Suddenly they saw someone. There, at the wide door opening into the veranda, they saw a small, stooping, blue-clad figure, the head down dropped, apparently seeing nothing. Her heart ceased its beating. Her body relaxed. Again the passion broke. Rodney rose to his feet hastily and turned away. She could even see his hand shake as it lit a cigarette and not feel his agitation because she was so relieved at the interruption. It would give her time. She must have time.

"Yes, Amah?" she said.

"It is eleven, my mistress, and your bath waits."

"That damned woman—" said Rodney under his breath.

"Always faithful—" Anne murmured.

"Can't you tell her to wait?"

"She wants to get home—she has a husband," said Anne. Somehow the sight of the drooping little figure there in the doorway gave her a wonderful feeling of stability, of support. She could think now, think what she must do. She would send Rodney away and think. She rose, very slender and self-contained, her reserve rising between them.

"I've been listening, Rodney, my dear," she said. "Believe me when I say I've been listening with all my mind—and heart—" she added softly. "I won't pretend that you haven't shaken me. I'm shaken as I've never been. I won't pretend that your—our love hasn't been the one thing. It has, easily —unless, perhaps—the baby—I don't know. I should even have to think about that. I don't—I haven't hidden from you that your understanding has been—everything, almost. I lean on you. If I should decide not to—I won't know how to go on living."

She paused, and he turned to her, his dark face alight. "Then, Anne—"

But she put out her hand to ward him off. "I wouldn't be truthful, Rodney, if I didn't go on and say this, too: that I have to think before I can decide. I have to decide whether I can leave Henry. He depends on me—you wouldn't believe how much—"

"I need you, too, Anne!"

"Perhaps, Rodney, but differently. I don't know how to say it. You need me to—to spend yourself upon. Henry needs me as a child needs his mother. Oh, dearest, let me think!"

"Anne, I'll always let you do what you want most—" he promised, but the light was out of his face. He was quite himself suddenly, dignified, a little cold. "Good night, then. Shall I come tomorrow?"

"If I send for you, Rodney."

"Very well, Anne." Their hands touched, and he was gone.

The small figure waited in the doorway. When the tall white man was gone she closed the door noiselessly and locked it, and waited until her mistress walked wearily up the stairs. Then muttering a little to herself she bolted the doors to the veranda, shut the piano, and turned out the lights and plodded up the stairs also.

Upstairs Anne undressed listlessly and stepped into the tub. The water was perfectly as she liked it on a hot night, cool but without chill. She stretched out her white body and lay full length, suddenly spent and utterly weary. She began to remember the evening, to remember Rodney, his every movement, how his voice had sounded. "All he said was true," she told herself passionately.

The Chinese woman came forward screened behind an immense towel. "Do not stay in the cool water too long, my mistress," she said in her little matter-of-fact voice. "It makes a chill in the bones."

Anne stepped obediently from the tub into the great towel. The woman wrapped it about her securely and slipped into the other room. There she stood waiting, her hands thrust into her sleeves. When Anne was seated before the dressing table, she took up the hairbrush and with steady, even strokes began to brush out her mistress's long brown hair.

Neither of them spoke. Anne staring into the mirror saw her own weary white face, and above it the wrinkled brown face of the Chinese woman. Once the woman looked into the mirror, met her mistress's eyes, and looked away again. Seeing that quick secret glance, Anne thought to herself uncomfortably, "I wonder what she thought when she saw Rodney kneeling and holding me like that." But under the hypnotism of the long, steady strokes she forgot her wonder and even her slight discomfort. The small brown face was bent absorbedly to the task. The woman did not look up again. Perhaps she had seen nothing, after all.

So Anne fell into a weary longing for Rodney that became, in the silence of the house, a sort of despair. She could not give him up. If he demanded her utterly, she would give up Henry. It must be so. She could not live without this tender love from Rodney. Why had she hesitated at all? Of course she would go with Rodney. All those two years it had been he in this dull little port city who had kept her contented and full of the feeling of the richness of life. Had it not been he who had taught her to see the beauty even in sordid streets? He had shown her a thousand lovelinesses, the touch of carving over a decrepit gate, the bit of jade on a child's necklace, the color of grain in the market, the light of evening upon an old pink temple wall. When she had first come and for years afterward she had seen no beauty among these strange people. Rodney had shown her all the secret beauties. With his eyes she had seen. Why had she thought they might go on and on this way? She realized for the first time how unfair she had been to Rodney—leaning on him, absorbing from him, and then giving herself to Henry. No wonder that he could bear it no more. Of course she must leave Henry.

It was decided. Her heart brimmed with exultation and a strange recklessness. What deep, romantic thing life might be for her yet! She felt the sudden necessity of speech to someone about it.

"Amah," she said, "if I must go away, will you come, too?"

The Chinese woman paused, the brush in midair. In the glass her little dark tragic eyes met the white woman's wide gray eyes. She asked, "You go away, my mistress?"

"Yes, yes, I am going away—to some other place. You've

been with me all these years. I want you to come with me."

"And the master?" Still the tragic small dark eyes fixed themselves unsmilingly upon the white woman's widened gray ones.

And Anne Page could not answer them. She bent her head somewhat and stirred in her chair, and made no answer. The Chinese woman began again her long, even strokes. At last she said in her little, toneless voice, "It is true I have served you all these years, my mistress, and I had thought none other would serve you, except I, so long as you were here in my land. I had rather serve you and live about your house than in any other place. To me this is heaven. This house is so clean, you are so kind. I have the memory also of the little beloved one whom I nursed, and whose body I washed when he was born and when he lived and at last when he died. We, you and I, we are bound together. But I cannot go, not even with you."

"Why not, Amah?" said Anne, touched, and suddenly wanting this woman with her always. "You have no children, you could go."

There was a pause. "I have my husband," said the woman simply. "I could not leave him."

"He has never done anything for you," said Anne. She remembered a wrinkled, filthy old man who came sometimes to the back door and asked for the Chinese woman. She remembered him, a man with a whining old face, and dirty hands. A swift comprehension came to her. "Why, I believe he smokes opium, even—that's where all your wages go!"

She stared accusingly at the brown face in the mirror, for the moment forgetting herself. "Amah, it would be better if you did leave such a wretch," she said with energy. "Has he ever supported you or done anything for you?"

"No," said the other woman quietly, "and what has that

to do with it, my mistress? Because he has done nothing for me shall I be evil also and do nothing for him? Is it so that a woman should be?" She brushed for a few minutes in silence. "It is true," she said at last, "that even from the first day of our marriage, I knew what he was. When I was brought a young bride to his bed I saw he was already an opium smoker. He was an only and beloved son, and he had learned to smoke from his own mother. At first I hated him. I hated him for a very long time. There were days when I kept a rope coiled in my bosom seeking for an hour when I might hang myself by a beam with it, if haply I were alone sometime. But I was never alone. They kept me working very hard always. And then I had children and I was not free—I could not die as I liked."

"And when the children died?" asked Anne somberly.

"By then," said the woman, patiently, "by then he had become like a child also to me. I had learned he could not do without me, and so again I could not die. Now I cannot die until he does, for I cannot leave him. He is used to our house, to his bed. If I prepare his opium every day, so much, and manage that he shall have no more, he does well enough and lives on. Every night when I leave you, my mistress, I set all in order for him and see that he eats something and has his tea. In the morning I do this also, and perhaps in the day a friend comes in. Once or twice he has grown dazed because he used his day's opium up too quickly and then he came in search of me here, as though I were his mother. And now I have a friend come in at midday and see that he has the portion for the latter half of the day, so that he does not become so confused."

The white woman stared into the mirror. But the brown face was tranquil and bowed over the task. "Has this been your whole life, Amah?" she asked, shocked into forgetfulness of herself, of Henry, of Rodney.

The little dark eyes looked up without a trace of self-pity. "What else?" she asked. "It has not been so bad. I have done all I should do. At night when I lie awake sometimes and grieve for my dead children I comfort myself saying, at least I have done all I know I ought to do. I cared for them though they died. If my husband has been less than a man, at least I have been a woman to him as best I could, and while I cannot say if there be gods who see us—I am only ignorant and do not know a single letter in a book—yet I can say this, that when I think of these things, even of my dead children, and how they died, though I tended them as best I could, and when I think of my man who has been more trouble to me than any child, and never any good, yet I am comforted and at peace in myself. I did what I could and so I do now, and so I cannot leave my man, not even for you, whom I love, my mistress. You are kind to me, and he is not. You would see me fed and clothed into old age, and if you go, I cannot hope to find another like you, and perhaps none will clothe and feed me when I am old. But I have him to clothe and care for until he dies."

"Do you love him?" asked Anne, staring at the quiet brown face.

"Love?" said the woman wondering, without lifting her eyes and keeping steadily to her task, "What is the word that I should have it on my lips? I never asked myself if I loved him even when I was young. How can I ask it now? It is not a word to be used by a woman like me. I have always known what I must do. When I do it, I am content. If I did not, I should be ill at ease in myself, and my heart could not rest."

There was silence and she began to braid the long brown hair. She went on softly, "It is like your own self, my mistress. The master comes home hungry and thirsty and he shouts aloud for you, and you go to him. You see that his clothes are laid out, and that he has his dinner as he likes it, and afterward you listen to him talk and he is eased and comforted. And when he is eased, I can see you are also, my mistress. It is the same with you as with me. Are we women not all alike? Only you are more fortunate than I in your fate. He is so good to you, the master. He never beats you as I used to be beaten, and he never curses you as my man still curses me, and he takes no other woman before you. You have everything, my mistress. He works for you and gives you money and you have silk garments and even jewels for your neck. You remember that green jewel hung on a gold chain which the master chose and bought for you once when he was away? I never had a jewel, nor even a coat I have not made for myself. Ah, it would be easy to be wife to a man like the master! He needs you every day, he cannot live without you, as even we who serve can see. He will not sit to eat unless you are there, even when he is hungry and thirsty after his work and play. Often when I have been weary with my life I think of this as a joy for me, that your life, my mistress, is so easy and so good and that the master is pleased with you. It is easy for you to serve him, and what but joy to do it? To serve—it is our lot. It would be a sad thing otherwise, for what would we do, we women? What more can we desire except to know that those whom we serve are happy?"

She sighed and pulled a few hairs from the comb and rolled them slowly about her brown finger. "I have talked too much," she said in apology. "I have wearied you. Lay yourself upon your bed and let me place the net aright."

Without a word the white woman lay upon the bed, and once more the little Chinese woman crept meticulously about the bed.

The white woman did not look at her. She stared toward the open window. A great dark red moon hung over the housetops. Henry would be asleep now upon the little junk, under that moon. She was glad she had put in his mat. It was so hot tonight. But at dawn it would cool. She worried an instant, wondering if he would wake to pull up the light blanket. Often at home he did not wake and she leaned over and covered him secretly. He slept like a child.

It was true. What would Henry do without her? What other woman could fill his need, even his simple, daily need, as she could? She had done it all these years until it was a part of her. No one could replace her—why it took years to make a wife! It was the work of her whole life, and how could she leave it? Suddenly she saw quite clearly that even enfolded in Rodney's tenderness she would think of Henry, lost without her, never able to find anything, his life in confusion. Even in the richness of Rodney's understanding she would long to order that confusion for Henry as she always had. When she thought of little Harry—and she daily thought of him—she would remember Henry, too, and wonder in pain if he needed to turn to her in his noisy, childlike grief. Why, it was almost as though Henry were little Harry, grown a man, but still needing her! And that was what Rodney would never understand, with all his understanding of her. What had happened to her in these few minutes? What change—what revulsion, what return to some great cosmic womanhood?

"I am not going away, Amah," she said suddenly, unexpectedly, almost to herself.

"Ah," said the brown woman softly. She straightened herself. Her task was finished. She opened the door and said, "Until tomorrow then, my mistress," and closed it softly.

Fool's Sacrifice

———————————

<small>SHANGHAI—1930S</small>

FREDDIE HILL WAITED alone at the dock in Shanghai for the ship which was to bring his wife from England. He stood very short and sturdy and thick in a crowd of dark agile Chinese, seeming not to see any of them. Nor did he see them. In the first place he did not notice Chinese, since long ago he had decided they looked alike and were a filthy lot. In the second place he was looking for his wife, Marian. She had been gone five months and he had missed her horribly—more this time than ever. There had been a steady dull ache in him for weeks; he hadn't even been able to take food properly, although that might have been the more than usually hot summer.

Still, over and over in the hot night when he had lain heavy and inert under the mosquito net, he had said to himself, "Jolly glad Marian isn't here," and he would picture her in the cool greenness of the rainy English summer. He saw her lying in her bed, her slender body delicately shaping the blankets under which she lay. Then he would remember that of course it wasn't night there now. While he was trying to sleep in the heat like a hot bath around him, in England it was day and she'd be walking probably, over the misty downs of Devon. Lots of rain that summer, she had written— she'd done a lot of walking. Well, he could see her thus too, very graceful in her green mackintosh, walking through the short heather, her dark hair blowing and curled.

Yes, and now she would come back, her cheeks all flushed

with English mists—good for her to get away once in a year or two, even if it did mean separation. It was always so nice to wait for her like this, knowing jolly well she'd be the prettiest woman on the ship—always was, and now prettier than ever, being one of those women who when they are girls are a bit awkward and long-legged, as she had been at eighteen when he'd married her, but when they were in their thirties were lovely and youthful looking. So was Marian.

Suddenly he saw her, all in white linen, standing by the rail. His heart gathered slowly into an immense pride and he stared at her solemnly and then raising his thick red hand waved it very stiffly. Around him chatter and laughter broke out as friends recognized each other, but he gazed steadily at Marian. She was prettier even than he remembered, leaning on the rail, smiling, smiling—a little white hat on her head. Lord, he'd forgotten how pretty she was when she smiled— her eyes as blue as anything—he could see her blue eyes now. She threw him a little kiss and kept on smiling. He waved once more stiffly, somewhat ashamed—always made him ashamed to show off anything in a crowd like this. The crowd was enormous now—people to meet their friends.

Nevertheless, he could not, when he got up the gangplank to her, refrain from putting his arm about her furtively and giving her a squeeze. It was then he noticed how thin she was.

"You're thin, aren't you, my girl?" he asked. She'd been thin when she went away, but England had always put some flesh on her. Now he could feel her delicate hipbone under his hand.

She moved a little restlessly from under it. "I am all right, Freddie," she said. "Kiss me, dear. Now for the bags. I *am* glad to be back again, Freddie dear!" And he forgot how thin she was in all the business of the bags, and in realizing afresh her beauty.

Nevertheless at dinner again that night, after Chang had finished serving them, he looked at her more carefully. He'd been hungry and had eaten well—everything tasted twice as good as it had when he was alone or even if he dined at the club with the fellows.

"This Mandarin fish," he had begun appreciatively over his tucked-in napkin.

"Isn't it delicious?" she interrupted him a little recklessly. "Almost as good as English trout." But even he had seen she had left half of her portion. And after the roast chicken Chang had asked anxiously, "Missie no likee?" And she had answered, "Very good, Chang, you tell cook very good." And to Freddie's astonished eyes she answered apologetically, "It was so hot in the ship, Freddie dear—the Red Sea—you can't imagine how hot it was. And we hadn't even a monsoon in the Indian Ocean—just too late, they said. I really wasn't cool for three weeks. It's taken my appetite. I'll be myself in a day or two."

"See that you are, my girl," he had answered seriously, and then forgot it again, for Chang had just brought in his favorite steamed pudding, full of figs.

At the end of his second helping he noticed to his real alarm that Marian had not even tasted this.

"I say," he said, very gravely indeed. "This won't do, you know—"

And then having taken the last bit, he really did sit back and look at her. She was wearing some sort of a thin blue thing, low-necked but with long sleeves, and she had put some pink stuff on her cheeks. Lord, she was pretty enough, but very thin—much too thin. The pink stuff didn't hide the hollows in her cheeks and the dress showed hollows in her throat.

"I say, Marian, you haven't been ill and not told me, have you?" he blurted. A thick anxiety gathered in his heart. He could feel it heavy in the pit of his stomach. "Shouldn't have eaten that last bit of pudding," he said solemnly.

"Shouldn't you, dear? I am sorry. Perhaps the hot coffee will help you," she said gently, rising as she spoke.

Then they'd gone into the drawing room and she had played a bit and he'd forgotten it again and then some friends had come in, the Staffords and the Browns, and they'd all got talking about England.

But when Mrs. Brown was going away she murmured to Freddie, "Dear Marian isn't looking so well, Fred. Has she been ill?"

This reminded him that at the table Marian hadn't answered his question. But he wasn't going to have Mrs. Brown talking—she was good, of course, but a talker. "Marian's not the kind that takes on fat, you know," he said somewhat gruffly. Mrs. Brown herself was very fat. She'd put on a stone in the last month. She always thought any woman thinner than she was too thin.

"No, quite," Mrs. Brown agreed. "Still, such dark circles—and *she* is quiet—much more quiet than usual."

Was she quiet? He hadn't noticed it. Well, he wasn't going to have Mrs. Brown noticing things. "Rotten trip," he said very noncommittally. "Beastly hot."

"It *was* hot," said Marian, smiling faintly. Ah, even he could see she was tired. He stared at her. The pink stuff stood out in patches on her cheeks, but her delicate lips were pale, and under her blue eyes the shadows were very deep. He hurried the guests off a little and closed the door firmly and locked it. "You go to bed now," he said vigorously. "You look tired as anything."

"I am tired—." She looked at him as though she had more to say and did not. He waited a minute, looking into her up-turned eyes. Was she *frightened?* What made her look at him so? But he imagined it, for she smiled and patted his arm, and they went up the stairs in silence, hand in hand, as they had done so many nights.

Now with her slender hand in his, alone with her at last after all the months, he felt a slow familiar warmth begin to steal into his blood. Lord, it was good to have her back, his wife back, alone together in their own home, the night before them. Other fellows he knew when their wives were gone acted like anything with other women—took regular flings, and no one thought the worse of them here in this damned foreign port. But somehow he couldn't. Once in a while he had gone to some dancing place with others and stared at the girls, but they seemed a tasteless lot and he couldn't do it, not when he'd had Marian and knew she was coming back. Fact was, he and Marian had been a bit of a laughingstock, he shouldn't be surprised, among their friends. Marian never looked at another man—never had, he knew. They'd been married young and had lived together fifteen years—no kids, but still liking each other best. He put his arm about her and held her to him with sudden roughness, and rubbed his square cheek against her neck.

"Glad to be back with your old Fred?" he mumbled against her delicious flesh.

He scarcely thought of the expected answer until he noticed its delay. "Yes—" she answered under her breath. Did she draw away a little? No, he imagined it. It was as it had always been. The thick heat was gathering in him now with urging. He could not wait.

And then when it was over, to his horror she turned and broke into silent weeping. He was so astonished he could not speak. At last he said in consternation, staring at her back, "Have I hurt you somehow, my girl?"

And she had answered passionately, "Ah, no, Freddie,

when did you ever hurt me?" And then she turned over again and bit her lips and looked at him waveringly, the light shining on her wet black lashes. "I am so tired, Freddie—terribly, terribly tired, somehow. Give me a few days."

"I'm sorry, my girl," he said humbly. "You should have told me."

"Oh, *no*, Freddie. It's all right. I just didn't realize how tired I was." She put up her hand and patted his cheek and kissed him once.

Then he had gone to his own room and she to sleep almost immediately, and he slept in his usual heavy fashion, only better than he had slept all summer. Once or twice he dreamed he heard her sobbing again and he stirred a little but not enough to waken. Besides, it was only dreaming.

So he had waited after that. He told himself he would wait until she made some sign of being rested and herself again. But he waited a week and a fortnight, and then a month passed, and still she made no sign. He began to think about this, as he had never thought about anything in his life, and at last it came to him slowly that something was different between them.

It was very hard to put one's finger on what was wrong. She'd get up in the morning very early, sometimes before he did, and be there waiting for him at breakfast. That was something new. She'd always used to have her breakfast in bed, and he'd come in and give her a good hug before he went to business, and carry with him the picture of her lying there, pretty as anything, on her pillow. She was always pretty in the morning, fresh, and her eyes blue as the bluest thing you could think of, and her hair all curly around her face.

Well, still it was rather nice having her at the breakfast table, too, very tidy in her street things. She was always going somewhere these days. There was that to wonder about. She was energetic even if she was tired, taking up a morning bridge club and teaching English in some school or other. In the old days she never would do any of these things women did to fill up their time. She liked reading and idling about the home. When he came home sometimes they'd go somewhere, but often as not she'd coax him and say, "Let's stay home. I have a new book," and she'd read to him a bit perhaps. Not that he understood what she read much. There was a fellow she used to read a lot—Lawrence or somebody, and it always sent him to sleep. He had never been much of a one himself to mess about inside people. He remembered she had got fearfully excited over a novel called *Women in Love*, and he tried a bit of it and it was beyond him—he didn't know what the fellow was driving at.

Or she'd play the piano. She played fairly well, people said, and he liked to hear her, although she always teased him by saying she could play the same thing every day and he never knew the difference so long as the piano made a noise. She liked to tease him. And of course he knew he wasn't up to her, not in such woman's things. A man couldn't potter about with such things if he had his way to make in business. She was clever, and he wasn't. Even at the club he had an idea the fellows didn't call him clever exactly. "Freddie's a good sort," they would say and clap him on the back, and then they'd laugh. Still, of course, they liked him, he knew, even if he wasn't clever.

Well, but now every day she wanted to go somewhere, and every evening it was guests or go somewhere. It was he now who wanted a quiet evening alone—he'd some sort of an idea he'd like just to sit a bit and hold her hand. Funny he didn't used to think of such a spoony thing, but now, waiting like this, he wanted just to be near her, to touch her in any way he could, even just helping her on with her coat was something. But she was so quick these days, so restless. She would answer him, her voice like a cry, "Ah, Freddie, let's go somewhere. I'm tired of the house." Tired! That was what she was always saying. Tired of everything, it seemed.

Then suddenly one night, after a month had slipped into two and winter was coming on, he had gone determinedly to her room and stood by her bed. A sort of sullen slow anger had been gathering in him. Tired, was she? Well, she'd been tired for two months and it was time enough. They were going back to their usual life.

She was already asleep, lying still, the covers about her shoulders, her long braid on the pillow. Or was she asleep? For when she felt his hands fumbling at the blankets, she cried out faintly as if he had been a strange man and then she said, gasping, "Freddie, don't—I'm so tired tonight!"

The slow anger in him broke. He jerked the covers away from her. "Tired!" he shouted. "That's all I hear. The truth is you're tired of your husband!"

What had made him say that he did not know. He'd never thought of such a thing. Weren't they happily married for fifteen years? He'd been perfectly happy, perfectly satisfied, "a lucky man" he'd said to her sometimes, and when she answered gaily, "I'm lucky too, Fred!" he had not disagreed with her. At such a time it seemed to him she was lucky. He had been a good husband. They were not rich but there was enough. She had servants and trips home. And he didn't run about with women when she was gone. Well, he rather fancied she *was* damned lucky, when he thought of some fellows he knew.

Now he flung these words at her. And she did not answer them. No, she lay looking at him, white as the pillow on which she lay, the night light shining faintly on her whiteness. And she answered nothing, only looked at him.

He sat down a little unsteadily on the bed. Was she not going to answer him then? His anger changed into a thick chill of fear. How queer she looked, lying there! Why, her face was hard, his wife's face! He'd never known before that when she stopped smiling or talking and just lay staring like that, her mouth was straight and hard. "I didn't mean it," he muttered and turned his head away. But she answered, staring at him, "It's true—it's true—it's true!"

That was what she had answered, his wife, his Marian! She said it just as coldly as that. He hadn't known what to answer. He just looked at her, unbelieving. He'd heard of chaps whose wives said such things—but not his wife—not to him, Freddie Hill. They'd been married fifteen years—

And then she had put up her two hands and pushed back the hair from her forehead, and she lay there and talked to him as she might have talked to a class at school, and she the schoolmistress, making her words plain and short, so he couldn't possibly misunderstand. No, no one could misunderstand what she said, even a man not very clever.

"Freddie, listen to me. You are never to come to me again in the night; never, do you understand? That's over. I thought I could come back and go on with the old life. I wanted to do right for you—to do my duty. I've been a good woman, Freddie. Time and time again other men have—and I've always refused. Freddie, you know how different we are. I don't blame you. I know you've done your best. But I have, too. I hadn't been married to you a week before I knew it was all wrong. But I'd married you and I was going to stand by you. And I did, Freddie. And I grew fond of you. Everybody *is* fond of you, Freddie. You're such a good sort."

She paused. He, stunned as he was, yet felt he must say something. So he muttered the thing her last words always brought to his mind, "Not very clever—"

"No, Freddie," she went on in this new, clear, firm, hard voice he did not know. "Not very clever. Not that I'd have cared for the cleverness, Freddie dear, if I could have loved you. But, you see, I couldn't. I was fond of you—I'm fond of you still—" She caught her breath and pressed her hands against her eyes. "Strange," she murmured as if to herself, "strange how with all this other feeling I am as fond of you as ever—only now I must not be touched."

At this a great dim light shone in his inner confusion.

"There's another fellow!" he whispered, shocked to his inmost soul.

"Yes—" she said, her hands still pressed against her eyes.

There was nothing for him to say to that, nothing at all. He waited, in complete confusion and dismay, seeing all his life rocking about him. At last she took her hands away and went on in the same clear voice, only now it was not so hard. Into her eyes had come a great pity, and she reached out and laid her hand lightly on his big thick hand. "Freddie dear, there's nothing to say except that this summer I met someone —we used to walk on the downs. And we both know how we feel— But I told him how good you are. Freddie—all our years together—I had to come back to you—carry on—I'm not the sort of woman—I can't just—" Her lips trembled and grew soft while he stared at them. "So there is no more to tell, Freddie dear. We said goodbye and I came back, and I can go on quite well, if only—you won't—touch me—" She pressed her hands to her eyes again and was silent.

Well, what had one to say? A clever man perhaps would know. But he was not clever. He stared at her hands pressed against her eyes, pressing the eyeballs in and in.

"Headache?" he asked at last.

"A little," she answered.

He rose and went to the table and fetched her bottle of eau de cologne, and opening the drawer found a clean handkerchief and very clumsily, for he had not done this before, he did what he had seen her Chinese maidservant do, wetting the handkerchief and touching her forehead. But even under this touch she winced and took the things from him and did it herself. But then she opened her eyes and smiled at him very sweetly.

"Dear Freddie!" she murmured. And after a hesitation took his hand. "Now you know everything. Don't talk to me at all about it, Freddie. Just let me alone awhile. And to bed now. There's a good boy."

Well, he would go, of course. He was back to doing as she said. He bent to kiss her good night, and then seeing the strange look in her eyes he straightened himself suddenly. She did not even want him to kiss her. Even he could see it.

"I hope your head will be better," he said, and marched very stiffly to his own room, remembering for once to close the door softly because of her head, and catching as he did so a glimpse of her face, smiling a little, quick, appreciating sad smile.

Well, he couldn't sleep, of course. A fellow couldn't sleep naturally on top of such a thing as this. He didn't know what to think about it at first. That other chap—he supposed he had to think about him. He wished he had thought to ask Marian what sort of a chap he was—probably a writer or artist or something. It came to him in a flash that sometimes when they'd met fellows like that Marian had seemed different—waked up, somehow, her face all lit up and her eyes shining like anything, as they didn't usually. Fact was, now he thought of it, she had rather a sad look naturally, eyelids a little drooping, mouth smiling but not merrily—just smiling. Still, he'd never thought her unhappy. He might ask about this fellow perhaps, except she had said she didn't want to talk.

Well, there was nothing to do, after all. She had been

sensible and come home. He must remember that he could trust her. An immense slow relief filled him. He could trust her. She wasn't like other women. Women went off half-cocked sometimes with any fellow. Look at that poor Jameson and his wife running off with a worthless Frenchman. People did silly things in these foreign countries, in ports like this even quite sensible, middle-class people like themselves did silly things. Of course Marian had come home, even if she had a bit of a fancy. Women did get these fancies. But she was back with him, chose to come back to him. After a while she would forget it. . . . And thus, lying very straight and still upon his bed and waiting patiently for sleep, sleep did come to him.

Yet the next morning, as soon as he woke, it was to a vague heavy sense of something wrong, and when he had waked fully, he remembered what it was. He got up very soberly then and shaved and took his cold shower and he did not go into Marian's room at all, though usually, if she were not asleep when he opened his door to see, he went in for her to look him over. But before he went into the dining room he stopped an instant, his hand on the door. He was suddenly shy of her this morning. What would he say? Would she be different? He waited a moment, and after thinking, decided he would say nothing if she did not.

So he went in and to his great relief found her quite herself, waiting for him, behind the coffeepot. He said good morning without kissing her and ate his American grapefruit. It was cooled and very good. So was his oatmeal good, and his rasher of bacon and his eggs. The coffee was perfect, and he ate rather more than usual of the muffins. Losing sleep made a fellow hungry. And while he ate she talked as she usually did of all she was going to do that day, bridge, luncheon with Mrs. Travers, music in the afternoon, guests to din-

ner tonight and they might go and dance afterward somewhere. He said nothing, not thinking of anything to say. He
was used to just enjoying Marian's talk! She put things so
interestingly.

"Full day," he answered and rose, just as he did on any
other morning, to fetch his things for business. Somehow the
whole affair seemed less today. After all, a good breakfast,
sunshine streaming in the window, the canary bird singing
like anything, a fire blazing in the grate, Marian so much herself, in fact, exactly like herself, everything was sure to be
all right.

Nevertheless, when he bent to kiss her goodbye since she
was so much herself there was that queer look in her eyes
again. She put up her lips, but he had caught the look first.
Good God, did she *hate* him? He was so startled he kissed
her forehead instead of her lips, and then stood above her hesitating. He must say something to that look. She had dropped
her head now and was very busy buttering a bit of the toast
she had taken and not eaten.

"I say, old girl," he began hurriedly, his heart pounding
slowly, "I only want to say I'll do anything I can."

She flashed him a deep look at that, and her lips quivered.
"I know, dear—thank you—" she said softly. He was warmed
by her voice, moved with a sympathy he could not understand, yearning over her—why, he loved her horribly! There
was nothing he wouldn't do for her. That other fellow
couldn't possibly love her as he did. Suddenly he had to
know something of that man. He began to speak thickly. "I
think you ought to tell me—I think it is due me—"

But she rose, her face instantly hard as stone. "What is due
you?" she said suddenly. Her blues eyes, always so deep and
soft under the dark lashes, were suddenly glittering, and
coldly clear. "Haven't I come back to you? You have had all

that is due you— When I think of all these years"—her hard-
ness broke and she was soft again, her face, her voice hushed
and quivering, her hands fluttering. "Don't talk, Freddie—
don't talk—*don't talk!* I—I can just bear it if you don't talk!"
And with that she had left the room quickly and he had gone
very soberly to business. Not at all comprehending what she
meant.

Well, what was a man to do then? He hadn't talked. They
went through that day and many days and they never talked.
That is, they didn't really talk. She was full of feeling about
this and that she was doing, but he became aware that there
were now two Marians, this one he knew, who came and
went in his house, made it cheerful and comfortable, filled it
with flowers and guests. This was Marian in the day.

But at night, after a swift good-night kiss, cold as snow
against his lips, she went into her room and shut the door,
and he went to his bed and lay, losing sleep every night
thinking about her—sometimes resentful, sometimes suppli-
cating thoughts, beginning to understand in his dim way,
since he was no more clever now than he ever was, that the
Marian in that room alone was not his Marian. In there was
a strange woman, thinking God only knew what thoughts,
writing letters, dreaming dreams—he did not know what she
was. Only sometimes this strange woman looked at him suddenly out of Marian's eyes if he forgot and came near her
with his hand. It was as if this other woman was always inside
his wife, guarding her body, guarding her soul, keeping her
away from him. It was too queer for him. He couldn't understand it, but it made him very uncomfortable, although most
of the time he could forget it, since Marian was in the day so
much herself.

Still, this sort of thing couldn't go on forever. At last he
was inclined to be angry with her again. Lying alone in bed

at night he had told himself this couldn't go on forever. He would tell her so and tell her the very next day. He wouldn't of course force her or anything like that—he was not, after all, quite so stupid. He would only reason with her, ask her if she wasn't getting over it. Wasn't it time they were really together again? He would begin very gently. So he did begin very gently. He said, the next day being Sunday and he at home by the fire in the upstairs sitting room and everything very cozy, catching her hand as she passed to put a bit of lettuce into the bird's cage, "It'll be nice when you come quite back to me, old girl. I'm getting jolly tired waiting."

He'd been as gentle as that. Where another man would have been rough and cried, "No more nonsense!" or something of that sort, he had been mild as anything. How could he have foreseen what she did? She rushed to the window and threw it up as though she were mad and cried out, "No, Fred, I can't—I can't ever— Look here, I'd kill myself—" And really for a moment he thought she would. He threw down his paper and went and jerked her away and pulled down the window and locked it, and then stood there speechless, shocked and astonished. And then she had fallen into a terrible fit of trembling and weeping, so that he hadn't known what to do with her because if he so much as touched her she shrank from him, and she cried out over and over again, "Oh, I'm so unhappy—don't touch me—I'm so unhappy—" and then had gone running to her room.

And he had sat a long time by the fire. It was a strange thing how suddenly the whole room was a different one. It had been a fine winter's morning, the sun shining in, the fire bright, the bird singing, the room warm and cozy and pretty, fresh flowers everywhere. He had been filled with comfort, thinking how nice it all was. And just because he had said a few words, the room was the dreariest place in the world.

Only that stupid bird would sing on, not knowing any better.

After a while it all came to him. She had been unhappy all along. All the time while he thought she was better, was getting over it, would be as she was before, she was unhappy. She would never get over it. No, she never would. He knew it now. No woman who looked at a man as she looked at him there by the window could ever get over it. What was it she had said about knowing the first week it was all a mistake? Then she'd never loved him at all. For now he knew she had never loved him. All the time he thought they were so happily married, so much happier than the other ones, she had been doing her duty, going through with her life. If he had been a more clever man, he would of course have seen it. He had, he now began to suspect, always been a bit of a fool. Another man would have seen what he had not, perhaps. Perhaps everybody had seen it except himself, he thought in complete heavy sadness. Of course he had never been worthy of her, of her brilliance, her beauty, her perfection as a wife. Good God, how dull he must have been for her all these years! Then remembering her as she stood before that open window he thought sorrowfully to himself, "I ought to be the one to die."

At last he could not bear the room and the silly cheerfulness of the bird, and he dared not go upstairs, and so he put on his topcoat and hat, and walked out into the streets. It was very bright everywhere, the streets filled with people, and a friend or two called to him. He nodded, his square face quite unmoved, and he walked on alone to the Bund, into the gardens, to a favorite spot of his where he could watch the boats upon the river. Here he sat upon a bench, staring gravely into the clay-yellow water, thinking what he would do now.

"She'll never be able to stick to me again, that's clear," he thought very humbly. "It's over. It's a pity I can't die and let her be free."

It would certainly be well if he could, say, seem to slip into the river. It was very swift there by the gardens, since it was near two forks into another river. Once at this very place he had seen an ocean liner drive into a Chinese junk and cut it straight in two. To his last day he'd never forget the way the junk slowly turned over on its side, and how the four Chinese sailors who manned it scrabbled like rats upon the wet bottom. But it was no good. The river was here a real whirlpool and it sucked them all down before even life-belts could be thrown from the liner. At the moment when the fourth one went under there was a great scream and a Chinese woman had leaped into the water and gone under the whirlpool too. She was the man's wife, come to bring his noon meal to him, and just in time to see the whole thing happen. . . . Well, if he could leap in like that it would be over as quickly.

But he couldn't. In the first place, he wasn't that sort of a fellow. He couldn't kill himself—silly thing to do, somehow. Besides, Marian was just the sort to take it very hard and feel it her fault and stay faithful to him dead as well as living, and it wouldn't be any good. Then he didn't know if his insurance for her would cover suicide, and he couldn't leave her penniless—that other chap mightn't have a penny, probably hadn't. The sort who ran with other fellows' wives usually didn't. Well, it was a muddle. He stared out at the water, whirling and yellow and vicious in the sunshine.

Then the thing came to him as easily as anything, really surprisingly easily for a fellow who wasn't clever. At that moment he'd seen Graves of the Tobacco Company come along with a girl—obviously a light girl, dressed up and painted like an actress. He'd got her for the day out of some place or other—rotten port was full of women like that. He couldn't stick them himself. Well, but there was an idea. It came to him as he answered Graves's gay salute with a solemn nod. He could tell Marian he had someone, too. That would set her free—free inside, that is, and it was the only freedom she'd take, being the decent sort she was. He'd be clever for once. Yes, he thought, with a great dull throb of pain, staring out over the cruel water, though it killed him as surely as though he leaped into that water, he would do it, and set her free.

So for a fool he was very clever. Therefore, through the rest of the winter into spring he went away at night alone very often, and he took care to make her hear him come in late. He spent Sunday afternoons sitting dully at his club instead of in his home where he longed to be. And when he came home he tried not to see her or care if she spoke or not, and she seemed not to care, either, where he had been, although he ached for her as he never had, and he yearned inarticulately over her silence and over her great eyes, too great in her thin face. She was growing very thin indeed, he thought. The days as early spring came on made her faint with their heat.

"You'd better get off to England early," he said gruffly one day at breakfast, not being able to stop looking at her pale face.

She looked up at him startled. "Oh, I shan't go this year," she answered quickly, flushing a little.

It came to him suddenly that here was a chance. Now he could finish his plan. "Been trying to tell you something," he muttered over his coffee cup. He could not look at her and tell this lie. He could feel her waiting.

"Yes?" she said gently. She was always so gentle to him these days. So polite.

"I want you to go to England," he said, setting down his

cup, and taking an enormous bite of toast. Then he blurted
it out. "Fact is, we'd better—separate. You go back to England and get your divorce—desertion'll do it—anything you
like—marry anybody you like—so'll I."

He chewed steadily, his big face very red. He could feel
her looking at him but he chewed on. He was glad now he
had a fat silly-looking face that always looked the same. No
one could ever tell anything from his face—happy or not, it
looked the same—a piece of meat was all it ever had been.
Well, he was glad it shielded him now.

"Why didn't you tell me before, Freddie?" he heard her
say softly. What was that note in her voice? Like singing it
was. How she'd been missing that fellow!

"Wasn't too sure myself until lately," he said. Still he
could not look at her. He ate on steadily. Then she spoke
again after a long silence, and he could feel her eyes on him.

"Well, Freddie, I am surprised of course. But I think—I
think I'd like to see her. Of course I know you've been—different all winter. I've wondered sometimes."

At this he was in a panic. What would he do? Then with
surprising quickness, almost as though he were a clever man,
he thought of the girl he had seen with Graves. Well, he
could hire a girl, too, hire her and tell her what to say, if he
had to do it. He planned it as swiftly as he could, chewing
very hard. But suddenly to his great relief she changed her
mind. "No, I don't want to—I think I'd rather not. Only—
are you sure you do love her, Freddie?"

He could feel her yearning over him a little, as a mother
over a child she had long cared for. She was scarcely able to
believe what he said. Yet believing, for, after all, he'd never
lied to her. Well, he must make her believe him still more.
He choked and nodded, his eyes still down. She was still looking at him, he knew. She began again.

"Do you love her terribly, Freddie? Do you feel you

couldn't live without her? Will she be good to you? Does she love you? Do you both feel you must—*you must*—are you sure, sure?"

The words poured from her and now he stopped chewing and he did look at her, forgetting himself. She was leaning toward him, her eyes lighted, her whole face lighted, her lips tender. He had never seen her look like this for him—never, never! She was thinking of that other fellow . . . Well, he'd done the right thing for her to set her free inside.

"Sure," he said steadily and took another bite of toast.

It was all over very quickly then. He had bought her ticket, and once more they were at the dock. There were friends this time—he hadn't wanted to come alone—women crying, "Lucky Marian to be going home again so soon!" Jim Brown said to him, "You're right to get her home before summer. She looks very seedy—been looking it for months. She doesn't stand the climate as my wife does." To all this he listened philosophically, getting her bags into the cabin, seeing to a box of chocolates he had bought, some books, all the usual things he did when she went to England.

And she went about like a woman in a dream. Whether she was happy or not he could not say, not being clever even at knowing her. He would have said perhaps, if he could, that she seemed not wildly happy so much as dazed, as one is dazed when a long enduring pain is suddenly gone, or a load unexpectedly removed. But she said no more about the other woman. She scarcely spoke at all.

Only at the last moment she took his coarse hand and held it for a moment between her two delicate palms and she then said earnestly, "You know I'll always be fond of you, Freddie. I'll always be the same. I'll never, never, forget you. You must write me and tell me how you are."

But to this he could promise nothing. He was not good at letters. Besides, what would there be to say now? There was nothing left in his life except going to his office. Of course one had to work. He gripped her hand and stared at her, his eyes swimming in tears. He hadn't had tears in his eyes, not since he was a kid. He loosed his hand quickly. But she had taken it again impulsively and put it to her breast, and cried out, "Ah, Freddie, I wish I could have loved you! And Freddie, you know I wouldn't ever have left you, no matter what, if you hadn't—learned to care about someone else!"

He was suddenly recalled to himself. He mustn't give himself away now, after all this trouble. He muttered, "I know that well enough, my girl—goodbye—" and he pulled his hand away quickly. Turning squarely without once looking back, he marched from the cabin and back to his empty house.

The Golden Bowl

NEW ENGLAND—1941-42

"BE PLEASED TO TELL ME, Honorable, if you will take your Japanese garments to America also," Ake said.

James Briony looked up from the books he was packing into a box which he saw would be too small for them. He had accumulated far too many books during these twenty years in Japan.

"Certainly, I will take those garments, Ake," he said. "Do I not spend my evenings in them?"

The bent, bowlegged little man who had been Briony's cook and valet for so many years nodded, lifted a dark silk robe, and began folding the sleeves carefully. No one could have foretold from his face that he felt anything. Yet five minutes later out of the subdued roar of the sea outside his window Briony heard a loud hoarse sob. He lifted his head and saw Ake's face wrinkled into a knot of weeping. Without a word, Ake, when he saw his master's eyes upon him, dropped the robe and fled from the room.

James Briony smiled sadly and went on with his packing. It was not the first time in these somber days of leave-taking that Ake out of apparent calm had burst into this childlike weeping. It was better not to notice it. To speak, to try to comfort him, made the weeping into hysteria. Unnoticed, Ake would come back in a little while to go on silently with his packing.

When the books were packed, what would he take next?

Briony asked himself. Five of the ten days he had given him before he must leave were already gone. He had five days left in which to pack what he could pack of his home, and what he could not pack into cases and boxes he must give away or destroy.

But there was so much he could not take and would not give away if he could. He lifted his dark, troubled eyes from the confusion of his study to the mountain that stood high above the clouds on the inland horizon. Thousands of times he had so lifted his eyes and had found help there in the snowy cone of Mount Fuji. This had been one of God's blessings on his lonely missionary life, that without any seeking on his part, he had been sent to a part of Japan where Fuji stood above the horizon. When years ago he had decided to have his own house, because he knew he would never marry Allis, he had found this bit of land near the sea. He had hired a Japanese carpenter to put up a small house of paper and wood which had looked frail, but had nevertheless withstood the years, the winds from the sea, and earthquakes. He had thought that of course he would die here. Instead, now, in the middle of his life, he was being returned to his own country, America.

For this he was totally unprepared. Other missionaries came and went across the ocean, but he had never left Japan except for a summer in China and another in Korea, in order that he might understand better the history of Japan.

"I wish I could take the mountain with me," he thought, and was for the first time thoroughly frightened. What would he do in that strange country of his when he lifted his eyes and there was no Fujiyama?

Allis, of course, was still in America. But whether she were even alive he did not know. They had not written to each other in these twenty years. He had destroyed those passionate love letters of hers the day he left America, a boy of twenty-four, still raw from the theological seminary. But then she had destroyed his. She had pushed them into the fire before his eyes when he would not put out his hand to take them that last day.

"I'm going to forget you and never think of you again," she had told him.

They were her last words and he had accepted them. He had taken up his round hat and left her, careful to walk slowly and erectly down the street. But the tears were running down his cheeks. He had gone on with his plans and in less than a week he was on his way to Japan. They were both very stubborn.

But he had made a life for himself. He could not perhaps have made it so satisfactory had it not been in Japan, so beautiful a country, in this village by the sea, whose people were kind to him. Yes, even now he understood that at heart they were still kind to him. If they dared not be kind openly it was because they had their children, their families, to consider. He could understand. They were being told that war with America was inevitable.

But he could not believe that Japan itself had changed to him. When he walked along the seashore nothing under his feet was changed. When he lifted his eyes there was the mountain in the sky, rosy at dawn and evening. He had a great deal of time to walk, now that the school was closed and the church closed to him. In the church Japanese Christians still gathered, but without him. "We have received orders," Mr. Hideyo, his assistant rector, said, and had taken over the services. Sitting alone in his study on Sunday mornings listening, mingled with the sound of the waves, he heard Japanese music coming from the open windows of the church next door instead of the old Christian songs—"Rock of Ages, Cleft for Me," "The Son of God Goes Forth to War."

War—how lightly the word sat upon men's tongues! It

ought never to be spoken aloud because of the curse it brought. He had in the last years seen the very look of his people change because of war being waged on China. A patient people, he had often thought in the old days, too patient with their arrogant police and little bureaucrats. He himself had been often annoyed with the petty police, watching his every movement, questioning where he went and why, and what was the smoke that came out of his chimney, and where he sent his letters and scores of such small things. But he suffered infinitely less than his people did, whose lives were under constant inspection. He wondered at their patience. Sometimes, he had thought, it seemed almost as though they enjoyed suffering and sacrifice. Certainly they grasped amazingly quickly the whole meaning of the suffering of Christ upon the cross.

He himself had not been able to grasp it so quickly. But then as a young man he had been headstrong and rebellious. Had Christ been less meek, more militant, the Christian religion might have prevailed more quickly. He himself was impatient with the will of another over him. He would obey only God's will.

It was the same headstrong quality in him which had refused to yield to Allis. But even in the beginning he had never wanted to love her. He had been angry at himself that he loved her. It was not as though he had been a young fool of a clergyman, unused to the world. He had not been reared only in parish schools and seminaries. No, he had grown up in a family of too many children but plenty of food and noise and fun. Over the house his strong dark-eyed Irish mother had presided with heartier noise than any of them, and he had loved his mother. It was she who had taught him to pray and to believe in God, she who had held his faith firm when he was young. When she died five years ago he had wept for the first time since he had come to Japan. His father had died years before, and he had sent his mother the share that all the children sent so that she could go on living in the white frame house where they had all been born and lived. The house was sold now. Not one of them could bear to go back to it when she no longer was there.

Loving his mother, why had he loved Allis? The two were utterly unlike—Allis, the only daughter of a rich man who played with horses for a life work; Allis, tall and blond, cool and used to her own way. But he had not given in to her—no, not even when they both knew how they loved each other. He had denied the love for a long time, denied it even to her. How she had laughed at him.

"You do love me," she had said, one summer morning, with that daring mischief in her blue eyes which terrified him because he was so weak before it.

"That I deny," he had said. He felt the cold sweat burst out on his brow, but he did not wipe it away.

"How can you lie to me with that surplice on?" she had demanded.

They were in the vestry of the church in Beechey where he had come to supply for the summer. He had come to the vestry before the service on a Sunday morning and she had followed him in, ostensibly to get a vase for the altar, for she had brought lilies from her garden. She looked very beautiful in her blue summer dress and wide white hat. He had seen this at once, and had felt it perhaps too deeply because of the quivering sensitiveness from which he always suffered before he preached. He had been very long at prayer that morning, and prayer opened the channels of the spirit. Sunshine, the summer air, the sounds of birds in the trees, the blue sea, everything had been too much for him. And then she had come in.

It was not the first time that they had spoken of love. But he had not spoken of it first . . . When he had accepted the summer season at a little seaside church who could have thought that Allis Earle would be there? He had thought of a quiet congregation of fisher folk, gathering every Sunday, whose homes he would visit during the week. He had not known that around Beechey were the homes of the very rich and that on Sundays there would be scattered through his small plain audience creatures who looked like orchids in a kitchen garden. They were the women who lived in the great timbered houses above the cliffs, who rode shining horses on trails through the pine woods. The men seldom came to church with them. He could not hide from himself as the summer went on that more and more of these women came on Sunday mornings. He avoided the shameful notion that they came because of him. When the first invitation reached his desk to a party he sent back his stiff regrets to— to—he had had to look at the letter again to see what the name was—Allis Earle.

She met him the next day on a country road as he was coming back from a call on old Mr. Lewis who was dying on the third farm back. She came cantering down the road toward him, seated on a great bronze-colored horse, her fair hair flying in the sea wind. He stepped out of the pebbly road so that she might pass, but instead she had reined in her horse and looked down at him.

"Why wouldn't you come to my party?" she demanded.

Then he knew who she was—Allis Earle. But he already knew her. He had seen her beautiful willful face in his church, Sunday after Sunday.

"I am very busy," he murmured.

"Nonsense," she said coolly. "You don't have to be any busier than you want to be in Beechey."

He had not answered this, and she leaned over to him.

"If I ask you again will you come?" she asked.

"No," he said, "I shall still be too busy."

That he hoped would make her angry. But instead she had laughed with great pleasure.

"You're too good-looking to be a preacher," she had said frankly, and touching her horse with her whip she had gone galloping off. He stared after her, confounded, and then she had swung herself around on her horse and seen him standing there like a fool, and had waved to him. He had gone on abruptly without answering her.

His good looks. They had been a curse to him always, from the time he had been a little boy and his mother had kissed him too often because he was so "pretty." That word had made him frown and purse out his lower lip, had kept his fists ready squared for a fight at any moment.

"Stop saying that!" he had shouted at his mother when his older brother had picked it up. "Pretty—pretty—" the boys had teased him at home and in school.

His mother had sobered at once. "Sure I'll stop, Jimmy," she said. "It's true you're too big to be pretty. I was wrong."

He began to grow when he was eleven and had grown steadily until he was six feet three. He had played football at college and been on the varsity team. But half the glory of it was lost when he was chosen the handsomest man in his class. By that time he had already decided to be a minister.

"Why are you a preacher?" Allis had demanded of him.

He had not yielded to her parties, but he had at last accepted the Sunday supper invitation when she said nobody would be there except her father.

But he was scarcely in the great door before he was sorry. He did not belong in a house like this. A wide, paneled hall stretched through the huge house and opened to the garden behind it. Beyond the garden was the blue background of the sea. Space and opulence, all that he had never had, all that he felt instinctively ought not to be, were here. What had he to do with such living?

And then Allis came out in a long white frock with full thin sleeves, her blond hair high on her head, and he had simply stood and stared at her.

"What is it?" she had asked, smiling and knowing very well.

"You are lovely," he had said impetuously. He had looked as any other young man might that night, for he did not like the signs of his calling. A man of God ought not to have to wear a livery, he always said. And then she had flung back her shining head and demanded of him why he was a minister.

He had tried to turn it off lightly. "That would take too long to tell," he had said.

But she had insisted, leading him as she talked toward a wide terrace. There were tables and chairs, a tray of glasses, and the evening light poured like music over the lavishly flowering garden. The sea was motionless, too blue, too smooth. Even the flowers looked too opulent, he remembered thinking. His mother had worked all her spare hours in springtimes over a border against the fence, but these flowers had been tended by many hands.

"That's why I asked you here alone," she said clearly. "I am curious."

"You mean, literally—there will be no one else here?" he asked alarmed. An evening alone with this beautiful girl— dared he subject himself to it?

"My father is in the house," she said. "He will be down for dinner after a while." She made a little face. "Don't be surprised if we quarrel," she said carelessly. "Our conversation is usually contradictions." She had leaned toward him, her hands clasped on her knee. He noticed her hands then for the first time, softly feminine, small, and extraordinarily delicate for so tall a woman. "Now tell me," she had said.

And to his own amazement he found himself telling her, as he never told even his own mother, how he had felt God's call upon him when he was seventeen, and how he had been led step by step toward the dedication of his life as a missionary. Those steps had been simple and clear. He had been a grave boy, full of young idealism and longing to live at his highest self. His mother had taught him to be in love with goodness, for goodness was beautiful and evil was ugly.

But he was masculine enough and he was not sure that his mother could have made goodness virile for him had he not when he was fifteen met Peter Grahame. Peter Grahame had been a missionary to Africa, a stalwart ruthless hunter of souls in the African jungle. In that hard sunburnt frame, in that militant outdoor Christianity, had been the harshness young Jim Briony had needed to show that a missionary could also be a man. He found himself telling Allis about Peter.

"I didn't like him," he said slowly. "You couldn't like him. There was a streak of cruelty in him. He could have killed a man, I think, for not believing in his creed. But he believed it himself. And he was willing to suffer anything. I saw from him that to believe anything with all one's heart meant willingness to suffer for it. That's what puts the muscle into religion."

"It's enormously interesting," she had said, without smiling. But what she was thinking was that here was the handsomest young man she had ever met and he was not thinking of her.

She set herself to make him think of her that night but he did not know it until she confessed it months later. By then they had told each other everything. But all that he had known that night was that he was thoroughly at ease and very comfortable and happy with this beautiful girl and the quiet, proud-looking man who was her father. It was true they quarreled, father and daughter, but with a glittering grace of speech. Laughter was quick, though its edges were sharp. But they were people of grace, and his love of beauty made him turn to them and confide in them. When he left the house that night he had felt constrained to say to Allis, "I am sorry I seemed rude at first—I mean, about coming here. I'm shy at parties—they're not for me. But this evening has been perfect."

She smiled without answer, and let him hold her pretty hand a moment while he spoke. Then she withdrew it so gently that he felt like a shock its exceeding softness. Even now, after twenty years, he could remember the touch of that softness in his palm.

Ake came back into the room, his eyelids red, and picked up the robe and folded it carefully and laid it in the trunk. The wind was rising and the roar of the sea was louder.

"When this war is over, sir, will you come back?" Ake inquired with indrawing breath.

"If I may," James Briony said.

"I shall be here," Ake whispered. "I shall return the house to you."

James Briony had arranged to leave the house to Ake and his wife and children. Why not? There was nothing in it but the simplest of furniture and Ake was clean to the bone and so were his family.

"I shall live with you, then," Briony said.

Would he ever return? His eyes seeking the mountain found no answer. There was a cloud over it, very dark. But if he could he would return here even if he were so old it would be only to die. Twenty years made a country part of one's being. He could not dig it out—no, not so long as the eyes of his memory held the picture of the mountain as it was on a clear day, a cone of snow against a blue sky. No one could take the mountain out of his brain. It was the mountain that had helped him to forget Allis's face at last. The sea would never have given him peace, but the unchanging mountain had given it. For years her face had sprung clear and living upon the surface of his memory and at such times he had steadily fixed his eyes on the mountain until its image had obliterated it.

Ake was taking something out of a box. It was a package wrapped in softly gilded paper.

"From your friends, sir," he said. "They did not dare to come here to give it to you, but they asked me to give it for them. There is a letter within."

He handed the package to Briony with both hands and with both hands Briony took it and unwrapped it. Within was a golden Satsuma bowl, very smooth and fine. Its surface was not decorated except for the faint etched outline of Fuji, touched at the crest with snow. Inside the bowl was the letter. It was written in the form of a poem, its brief unrhymed lines brushed on rice paper.

> An empty bowl
> Holds what cannot be seen
> By enemies.
> But friends perceive
> The bowl is brimming.

"Tell them—it is beautiful," he said to Ake. He felt moved and comforted. He put the letter in the bowl and wrapped the paper about it again. "How shall I take it without breaking?" he asked.

"You must carry it in your hand," Ake said.

So it was that he reached the shores of his own country carrying in his hand a golden bowl. No one had come to see him off the day he left his home except Ake, who carried his bag. He had not expected anyone, and yet he realized as the train made ready to leave the station that he had hoped some few of his church members might have managed to stroll by the platform at that moment. Mr. Kato, perhaps, with whom he had spent so many hours of good talk beside the charcoal brazier in winter or in the garden in summer. Mr. Kato had been his warm friend for nineteen out of twenty years, and had all but built the church whose pulpit was planned to face the long window looking out upon the mountains. The memory of those Sunday mornings when above the devout black heads of his quiet congregation he saw the mountain in the sky above was now like a dream of heaven to him.

Two days later, hours out at sea from Yokohama, he had stayed on deck for a last sight of the mountain. He was not superstitious, but he had fixed his eyes on the mountain. It was covered with a light gray cloud, and his heart sank. There was an old saying that if when one departed the mountain were hidden, he would never see it again. He had leaned upon the ship's railing, watching that cloud. Would it move, would it shift, before the ship went on? Quite alone as he was, it seemed to him that if at least he could see the mountain, he would be comforted. For half an hour he had stood there, while passengers came and went on the decks. The cloud had not lifted, it did not lift, until suddenly at the last moment he saw it fade. It was the sun that made it fade, the evening sun, clearing the sky before it set. He knew the reason was natural enough and yet it was a miracle. At the last possible moment, Fuji shone upon him, a clear and snowy shape.

"I thank Thee, God," he had whispered, gazing upon that shape.

Now in San Francisco he held his golden bowl firmly in his arm as he stood by his box of books, waiting for the customs examination.

"Japan, eh?" the customs man growled. "Well, I guess you're glad to be out of there!"

He glanced with kindly contempt at James Briony's tall, slightly stooping figure.

"Books, hey?" he muttered when he had pried off the lid. "Japanese? You read 'em?"

"Yes," James Briony said.

"What's that under your arm?" the man demanded.

"A gift," Briony said, and unwrapped it.

In the sunshine of an unusually clear San Francisco morning the golden bowl gleamed.

"Say, you'll have to pay on that," the man exclaimed. "It must be worth a lot."

"It is," Briony said, "but I don't intend to sell it."

Later in the shabby hotel room which was all he could afford, he put the bowl on the table and stood looking at it for a moment. Then he could not bear its incongruity. It seemed to him an insult to beauty to expose it in such surroundings, and he wrapped it up again and put it on the shelf in the closet.

He did not unwrap it for a week after that and then it was in the boarding house in Beechey. He had come to Beechey by instinct, feeling the necessity to return to the one spot that now seemed familiar to him in his own country. He shrank from meeting his brothers and sisters. He had not seen them in all these years and they had written fewer and fewer letters, and now he had not even told them he was coming, lest he seem to be dependent on them. The white house of his childhood was empty. He must somehow make acquaintance again with this country of his and to accomplish this he must start from something he already knew. Sitting by the window of the train across the country, he gazed at forgotten mountains and rivers and towns and at people strange to him though they were his own in race and ancestry. Japan had stolen something from him, something American that he must regain again. Where would he find it? His mind, searching the scene for a spot that could for the moment seem home, had lighted upon the memory of Beechey. The sea would be there, at least. He was used to the sea. But there would be no mountain.

He had put the idea of Beechey away from him at first. No, he would not go there where Allis and he had once loved each other through a passionate summer. He was stern with himself. Because he was desperately alone for the moment he must not remember something that was dead and forgotten—or if he remembered, let him remember what Allis had said.

"I don't want you to go to Japan," she had said.

It had not occurred to him in those days that she would not want to go to Japan with him.

"I want to live in my own country," she had said.

"But, Allis, you don't mean you want me to give up—my work?" he had asked.

"You can preach here, beloved," she had said.

She was not a woman to use the words of love lightly, and half the meaning of what she had just said was lost for him because with it she had called him "beloved."

But she had meant what she said. He found that out as the days passed. It came to him fully one Saturday in late August that she had no intention, however much she loved him, of being a missionary's wife, and that she had only waited to make sure of the depth of his love before she told him so. He had sinned that August morning in leaving his sermon half-finished to walk with her. There along the seashore where he had thrown himself beside her on the sand he was punished.

"I love you more than anything," he had told her, forgetting God. The beat of the sea was like his own heart that day. He took her soft hand and pressed his lips into the palm.

Her beautiful face looked down upon him from under a wide white hat. Her blue eyes grew grave.

"Then—give up Japan," she had said.

He got up then to his knees, still holding her hand. "Allis, do you—do you—" he was stammering. "Are you asking me to—to?"

"Yes," she had said clearly, "I am asking you to choose between Japan and me. For I won't go to Japan, Jim—I've made up my mind."

"But, dearest, you'll be with me—my wife!"

She shook her head, and he dropped her hand and rose to his feet and stood looking down at her. "Do you mean—you'd let me go without you?" he demanded.

The sea whirled at their feet as though with laughter.

"Would you go without me?" she asked.

He looked away. He could not answer. Then without a word he had turned and left her. He strode through the sunshine back to the solitary little manse and threw himself on his knees for a long time. But he did not pray. He knelt there thinking what it would be like to live without her. Then when he knew he rose and wrote a new sermon. It was the best he had ever preached. The next morning the little congregation in the church saw him come in like a young archangel in his robes, and they listened to him while he told them that whoever would not leave father and mother, wife and child, for Christ's sake was not worthy of Him. He did not once look at Allis, but he knew that she sat there beneath him, her face upturned to his.

When he had finished he went back to the manse exhausted and could neither eat nor sleep. Had God softened her heart? He cursed himself that he thought of her and her only, and hoped that what he had said could have changed her.

For this he was punished by a letter which she sent him that afternoon. He heard a knock on the door and when he went to it there was her chauffeur.

"Miss Earle told me to give this to you, sir," the man said. He tipped his hat and went away and Briony stood there holding the note. Then he took it into his study and shut the door behind him. He sat down, the note in his hand.

"I must be prepared for anything," he told himself. But when he saw the note he knew he was not prepared.

"There was no use your preaching at me," she wrote in her distinct handwriting. "I will not go. If you will not stay, then I suppose we don't love each other enough."

He had not slept when he went to her the next morning, mad for her, ready to promise anything. But suddenly God had saved him. On the way to her house, as he walked along the shore beside a calm and windless sea, alone, like Saul he saw a vision. It was a vision of himself and what he would be if he gave up himself to a woman, even to her whom he loved. His soul would die. He knelt in the sand, beside a gray rock, and gave his promise to God that he would do his duty. When he rose he felt strong and at peace. He could have lain down and slept after the bitter wakeful night.

But he did not. He went on to her house and asked to see her and she had come downstairs, a little pale but very beautiful, very resolute. In her hand were his letters, the letters he had written her although he had seen her almost every day. There was a drift-wood fire burning on the hearth in the room where he waited for her. When she saw the sternness of his face she walked swiftly to it and dropped the letters in the flames.

Everything came back to him now as he woke in his first morning in Beechey. There was no one in the boarding house whom he knew and indeed almost no one anyway at this season. He saw that when he went downstairs to breakfast. He sat down alone at a small table and ate frugally of what was set before him, and rose without having spoken to anyone, and then his hat in his hand he went outdoors. It was late autumn and the trees were leafless and the town looked silent and sad. Sea and sky were an even gray. He walked toward the church. The door was open and the janitor was sweeping the porch. He stood looking about him. In twenty years the church was not changed at all. There was still the smell of the sea in it that he remembered. The janitor looked at him and did not speak. He was a small stooping man with a long, stained moustache, and he was in his shirt sleeves and vest.

"Who is the minister here now?" Briony asked.

"We don't have a reg'lar one," the man replied, "only in the summer, when the town folks are here."

Briony bit back the question that flew to his lips. No, he would not ask of Allis. He had not come back for her.

"I preached here once," he said gently.

"Yeah?" the man asked without interest. Then he stopped as though he had an idea.

"You still a preacher?"

"Oh, yes," Briony said, "though I have been a long time out of this country."

"Lookin' for a job?"

"I suppose—yes, in a sense. I must find a place of some sort for myself."

"Why don't you ask the session for a try?"

"Here?"

"Where else would I be talkin' of?" the man retorted. He spat into the pile of dust and stared around the small churchyard. "Things are pickin' up with the war in Europe," he said. "People get money and the next thing is wickedness. They'd better be hirin' a preacher and payin' his salary to get 'em to heaven instead of goin' their own way to hell."

Briony laughed. "There's something to that," he said. He buttoned his coat about him. The salt wind was cold. "But I don't know that I could preach to Americans anymore. I've been away for half a lifetime."

"Furrin' parts?" the janitor asked, leaning on his broom.

"Japan." James Briony said.

The old man whistled. "Say! Did they torture you over there? I hear they're kind of mean."

"Not at all," Briony answered. No, not unless you could call his final utter isolation torture.

"Well, I reckon you're glad to be home," the old janitor said, beginning to sweep the steps.

"Yes, I suppose I am," James Briony said. He stepped over a pile of leaves and went away, turning over in his mind the possibility of preaching here in this church where he had first seen Allis.

But he came to no decision for days and weeks. He hesitated to promise to stay in Beechey when at any moment the fog in the world might clear and he could go back to Japan, where his real congregation was. He had a year of furlough—there was no haste even for a job. He walked a great deal, usually by the sea, read far into every night, and thought much. His life, he now realized, had been very solitary. His Japanese friends had been precious to him with their gentle, precise ways of courtesy, but none of them had come into the innermost parts of his being. He was fond of them—there was scarcely a day still when he did not miss Ake and he thought often of Mr. Kato and of his family, and of the Oyama family and the Matsuboto family—houses where after a long time of knowing only the men he had at last been trusted enough to enter. He had eaten with these families and had sat by their braziers in winter and wandered in their gardens in summer, examining with them the perfections of their shrubs and stones and mosses. To none of them now was he changed, nor could he feel them changed to him. Rather it was as though all of Japan were static and waiting. When he went back he would find everything just the same.

Because he still expected at any moment to go back he could not become a part of Beechey. He came to know faces very well, to speak to some, to nod to others. But he did not know anyone. He might have gone away and did not. Where did he know anyone better?

Once on a shining still afternoon in early winter, led by his memory, he had walked to the house where he had known Allis. He stood for a long time gazing at it. Nothing had changed except that the trees had grown enormous, and now the house was half hidden by them. As he stood there a gardener came out from a great clump of beach plum and began to rake up leaves. He glanced at Briony and did not speak. But Briony was used to silence now from Beechey. He waited until the man was near and then he said affably, "I came to look at this house because I visited here as a young man."

"Used to know the family?" the man inquired, stopping to lean on his rake.

"Somewhat," Briony said and then added, "in fact, rather well."

"Nobody's left now but the daughter of the old man," the man said. "Allis, they call her. She comes here years she don't go to Europe."

"I suppose nobody will go to Europe this year," Briony said.

"Reckon not," the man said. He moved away with his rake, and Briony walked on. But the sight of the house had stirred his heart. Allis had been so beautiful a girl, fresh to see, sweet—he remembered still how sweet was the odor of her hair.

That had been a Saturday. The next day, sitting in his room alone and manipulating a new radio he had bought, the first he had ever owned, he had released a loud and excited voice, breaking across the score of a ball game, breaking across music and an endless family serial:

"Japanese planes—Japanese planes—bombing Pearl Harbor!"

He shouted in horror and gripped his knees. It could not be true—it was impossible—the Japanese would never do such a thing! They were so meticulously careful in their—their human relationships—the war in China—he had always thought half he heard about it was not true. The Japanese whom he knew could never do such things—

"More news in fifteen minutes," the voice screamed, "Keep tuned in, folks!"

But suddenly he could not endure being alone. He turned off the radio and hurried into the parlor of the boarding house. There was no one there and he went outside. The peace of Sunday was already broken. People had been listening to their radios. Men were hurrying out of their houses. Under the trees in front of the church steps a small crowd of fisher folk was gathering.

He went up to them in his agitation. "I am sure it can't be true," he said. "It's a mistake."

But the faces they turned to him were grim.

"Reckon it's true," a man said.

"Reckon it is," others agreed.

"Well, them Japs have had something comin' to 'em for a long time," the man said.

"This means war," a man named Jacobs said. He turned as he spoke and stared out to sea, and they all turned with him

and gazed over water so blue it looked solid enough to walk
upon.

"I was in the last war," he said slowly. "Submarines come
right up to the reef yonder. Stuff washed up on the beach—
bits of lifeboats and such, and dead bodies."

By night Briony knew it was true. He sat for a long time,
the radio turned off. In the shadowy room the golden bowl
shone softly from the mantelpiece. He fixed his eyes upon it.

"What I remember is still true too," he thought.

But there was no going back to that memory. The next
day he applied for the church in Beechey and after two days
he was accepted, and so he moved into the manse again.

"That's a pretty bowl," young Mrs. Capey said, hushing
her baby on her shoulder. The baby was to be christened
this Sunday morning in May, and she and Mr. Capey were in
the vestry, waiting to go in. James Briony smiled.

"That is a very special bowl," he said. "I shall tell about it
at the service. Shall we go in?"

"Oh, I'm so nervous," Mrs. Capey breathed. "I hope the
baby'll be good."

"I guess the folks have seen babies babtized before this,"
Mr. Capey said. He was a young ship carpenter of a solid
build, his hair burned white in wind and sun and his face red.
In his Sunday suit of dark blue he looked as though he had
blocked himself out of his own wood. He clucked at his
four-month-old son, and the baby stared at him without
smiling.

"He looks a very good baby," James Briony said. It was
his first christening, and this morning it had come to him, as
he left the living room of the small manse, that he would take
his golden bowl for a christening bowl. Could there be a better symbol for a little child about to begin his life in the war-

ring world? He knew now it would be a long war. Two ships had already gone down off the coast, torpedoed by enemy submarines. He had read a burial service over the body of a young man whose head was crushed when he washed in, dead. He would not at night forget that boy. They had never found his name.

He was glad this morning that he had a baptism and not a burial. He led the way into the church and there the congregation, staying after the Sunday morning service, rose, according to an old Beechey custom, to greet the child about to come into the congregation through the promises of its parents. James Briony, very tall in his robes, moved to the front of the chancel and when the child was before him he took up the golden bowl.

"This bowl," he began in his mellow kindly voice which reached easily to the uttermost corner of the old church, "is a sacred bowl. It is a bowl of friendship, given to me by those who are now our enemies. But before God, who are our enemies?"

So he proceeded in his few finely chosen words to tell them how this bowl had come to be his. "May this child," he said in grave conclusion, "be consecrated to that divine friendship between human beings, which, recognizing no barriers of race or nation or creed, reaches into the hearts of men and women all over the world and unites them in a common humanity."

He did not notice the stir and whisper that went over the congregation, nor did he notice the quick look that passed between the young couple. Absorbed in the rite, he dipped his fingers into the water in the golden bowl and touched the child's head with it and began to pray.

That night as he sat in his study reading a book of Japanese poetry, the doorbell rang. He was alone, for Mrs. Hardman, his housekeeper, who slept in, was out tonight, and for his ease he had put on his Japanese robe, remembering as he always did, Ake, who had asked whether he would wear it again. He wore it often. Now he put down his book, listened, and heard the doorbell again. He rose and went to the door and there was Captain Jackson, the master of a fleet of fishing boats.

"Come in, Captain," he said heartily. "This is very good of you. I don't often have company on a Sunday night."

Captain Jackson coughed behind his huge hand, stared at him, and came in without answer. But silence, James Briony had discovered, meant nothing in Beechey. When a man had nothing to say, he said nothing. If he had something, he waited until he was ready to say it.

"Come into the study," he said, cheerfully. "I was reading. On Sunday nights I find it rests me."

Captain Jackson came in and sat down, his hat hanging in his hands between his knees. He still had on his Sunday clothes, and his gray beard was freshly trimmed.

"I come around," he said slowly, staring at the Japanese robe, "thinkin' I ought to tell you before you hear it otherwise that the folks have been doing some talking today."

"Yes?" James Briony said. He had been minister in the church now for six months, and it was not the first time that Jackson had come solemnly to tell him what "the folks" were saying. He was grateful, for it prepared him for his vestry meetings the next Wednesday before prayer meeting, when in measured, official terms, he heard the same things from his vestrymen.

"They don't like your babtisin' the Capey baby out'n a Jap bowl—seems like it would mean bad luck," he said. "Course that's silly," he added when he saw Briony's astonished eyes, "but you know how folks are. Seems that Lorries was countin' on babtisin' their baby soon, but they say now

they won't do it if you're goin' to do it out'n that bowl. And
Capeys been talking about they don't know if it could be
called a Christian babtisin' or not. Ever'body says it's queer
when we got a real silver christenin' bowl that the Ladies Aid
paid for that you wouldn't use it."

"Well!" James Briony cried. The golden bowl stood on
the mantelpiece—he had not taken it back to the living room
this morning. It shone softly gold and pure in its shape, the
faint etching of Mount Fuji upon its surface clear in the
light. "How very absurd!" he said sharply.

"Course I don't believe in bad luck like that," Captain
Jackson said, reflectively. "Tisn't that I mind."

"What do you mind, Mr. Jackson?" James Briony asked
gently.

"I think we oughtn't to use enemy things now when we're
at war—it's the idea that ain't fitten," he said, "not, not with
tankers bein' sunk right at our front yards, you might say."

"I see," Briony said. He suddenly felt as remote from Mr.
Jackson and from Beechey as though at this moment he were
still in Japan. A wave of bitter homesickness went over him
for that little house at the foot of Fuji. He passed his hand
over his forehead. "Tell them I won't ever use the bowl
again," he said. "Tell them I will keep it for myself. I wanted
to share it with them—all the friendship it holds." He quoted
the verse that had lain in it when it was given to him.

Captain Jackson listened and coughed. "Yes—well, I guess
I'll be goin', Dr. Briony," he said. "Monday mornin' comes
about as quick as I hit the bed Sunday nights. And the fishin'
boats come in early these days."

He rose and put out his hand and James Briony took it. It
was a hard but kindly hand.

"That was a real good sermon you preached today, sir—
folks like your sermons most of the time," Captain Jackson
said.

"Thank you," Briony said.

He closed the door behind his visitor and locked it. Then he went back to his study and sat down again in the old easy chair which had held so many of his predecessors and gazed at the golden bowl. It was the only beautiful thing he owned. Let others hate it if they would but he could not hate that which he loved. For him the golden bowl was still brimming.

He carried the feeling of loneliness through the night and woke with it in the morning, and remembered it as an evil dream. He tried to shake it off as he bathed and dressed and had his breakfast. Monday morning was always a low point after Sunday. But it was a glorious day. The sunshine of late May poured through the apple trees outside his window and fell across the table in a pattern like latticed Japanese windows. From his window here he could not see the ocean and the land was calm.

"I'm going for a walk, Mrs. Hardman," he said, smiling faintly as she came in with his coffee. "If anybody calls tell them I'll be back within the hour."

"Monday mornin' folks'll be too busy to think to call you, I reckon," Mrs. Hardman said heavily. She poured the coffee and set the pot on the table beside him and went out. She was a stolid, thickly built woman, a widow, inclined to gloom and silence but very clean. He had got used to cleanliness in Japan, and had to have it. Whatever gossip she heard she never brought it into the manse to him, and for that he was grateful. If she had heard the talk yesterday about the golden bowl, she would not let him know.

He rose after a few minutes and went out, wearing no hat, and his hands in his pockets he sauntered down the road at the back of the manse. It was a narrow country road, leading away from the beach into wooded hills, and it was his escape into what he called, to himself, "free country." Almost never did he meet anyone there.

But this morning when he had walked perhaps half a mile he saw a copper-brown horse cantering toward him. His heart stopped before his feet. Then he made himself walk on. If it were Allis, then they would meet, as it was, indeed, inevitable that they should meet. All through the spring he had known that as summer came on they must meet. He had wondered a little sometimes, unwillingly, how it would be to see her again. But he had put the wonder away as idle. They were not the same two people who had once wanted to marry each other. He was a middle-aged man, not a little tired and lonely, and she—she was not much younger than he. They could meet gravely and with calmness, with nothing between them except the slight discomfort of memory.

He stood still, forgetting to walk as the horse cantered near. It was she—there was not the slightest doubt. She wore a brown habit and no hat, and her fair hair was flying in the wind which blew in from the sea. From this distance she looked exactly as she had looked, tall, slight, sitting straight on her horse, her head flung up. He did not move, and she reined in her horse sharply.

"Do you want me to run over you?" she called in her clear voice.

"You may, if you like," he said.

She leaned over her horse's mane and he saw the recognition in her eyes.

"It can't be you," she exclaimed. "I didn't believe you were here even when I heard it."

"Why not?" he asked, hating himself for the hot red he felt creeping up his cheeks.

"Because you're in Japan," she said.

"I've been here for six months," he said.

"Doing what?" she demanded.

"My old job."

"Still preaching!"

He nodded, and she slipped from her horse, and put the reins over her arm and came toward him and held out her hand. He grasped it, and felt it as it always had been, narrow and soft. But he saw now that she was older, as slender as ever in body, but her fair hair was graying, and her fine high-colored skin was wrinkled a little about the eyes. Youth was gone from her face, though she was as handsome as ever. What had been too decided in her youth was now natural and becoming and not too much. And her eyes were still splendid, blue as ocean water under sun. Their handclasp was firm but brief and then they stood frankly looking at each other.

"So they made you get out of Japan," she exclaimed. "I know you wouldn't have come home otherwise."

"You are right," he agreed.

"How does it seem here?"

"Quiet," he said.

She tapped her boot with her whip. "Why did you come to Beechey? I should think there'd have been other places more interesting."

They began to walk up the lane toward the manse, not with any purpose, but because she could not stand still. Without knowing that he remembered her restlessness, he did remember, and unconsciously he had begun to walk with her.

"I have no home anymore," he said. "My parents are dead and I haven't seen my brothers and sisters in so many years that I'm afraid to go and find them now. I came to Beechey almost by instinct—and found the church needed a minister, and stayed."

"You never married?" she asked abruptly.

"No," he said.

"Nor I," she said shortly and laughed. "Not because I couldn't have or didn't want to—but because I didn't dare."

"Is there anything you don't dare?" he asked with his faint smile.

"My father played me a nice trick," she said bitterly. "Do you remember how he and I used to fight? Somehow we fought more after you went away. Oh, I was beastly, I know! Well, when he died he took his revenge. He believed in women staying in the home, you know—obeying their husbands, and all that. We used to fight about that, too. Can you imagine what his will was?"

"How can I?" he replied.

"No one could," she retorted. "But what a pretty revenge! I've had to admire it as pure revenge, even in my rage at him. He left all his money, Jim, in trust—to my husband, to be administered for me. I have the income—but my husband has the estate. So—I haven't taken a husband. That's been my revenge. But it's not so successful as his."

He did not answer because he could not. She walked along slapping the side of her boot with her whip, her face bitterly smiling.

"I don't quite see—" he began.

But she cut him off. "How would I imagine that any man loved me for myself after that? Why, I wouldn't have trusted even you!"

"I wouldn't have wanted to marry you under such circumstances," Briony said deliberately. She threw him a look and he caught it and she laughed.

"There—you see!" she cried. "No decent man would."

She walked more quickly and he felt her immense restlessness and still unspent energy. He glanced at her and was struck by the beautiful bold profile. Yes, she was more beautiful than she had ever been, and more magnetic. The years had added and not taken away.

"That manse," she said suddenly, "it hasn't changed a bit."

"If the furniture wore out they've found more that seems

to look just like it," he admitted, "but I think they have re-papered the walls."

"You aren't going to stay there?" she exclaimed.

"Why not?" he asked.

"But now," she urged, "with the country at war, and everybody working! Why, even I, though I don't look it, am fearfully busy."

"What do you do?" he asked.

"A dozen things," she replied. "But I don't want to talk about them now. I came here to get away from them."

Over their heads the trees met and under their feet were sunshine and shadows. The air was fragrant around them. He could not repress a sudden lift of his heart.

"I don't know if you are as glad to see me as I am to see you, Allis. I—I didn't know how I would feel meeting you again, but I'm glad."

Her eyes grew warm. "That's nice of you, Jim," she said. "Of course I'm glad to meet you. But I knew I'd be glad—unless you'd grown Japanese or something. I could always be myself with you. I value that more than anything else."

Without loving her at all he felt close to her, as he might to someone whom he had once known very well and come back to now. All of the heat had gone out of them and only what was solid and true remained. They liked each other. He liked her honesty and she liked his.

"Will you come in awhile?" he asked. "I think Mrs. Hard-man is there."

"No, I won't," she said, smiling. "It would please Beechey too much. But I'll come to church Sunday and maybe after a week or two I'll ask the minister to come to tea—as I always do. I've had a dozen ministers to tea in the last twenty years. They don't seem to stay here very long. But then most of them have had lots of children."

"The manse suits a single man better," he said.

They were facing the sea as they walked and suddenly she lifted her whip.

"Look!" she cried.

He looked and saw a flame leap high upon the horizon of the ocean.

"A ship!" he cried and began to run. She slipped the reins over a branch of a tree and followed him. People were gathering from the village upon the beach. They turned and stared at them half-curiously as they came up together. But no curiosity lasted while that angry fire burned. Towers of black and oily smoke rose into the sky and red flames slid out over the water. From the coast guard station five miles down the beach small boats were putting out.

"That's three ships down," Captain Jackson said grimly out of the crowd.

Briony, watching, was ashamed that he was still hotly conscious of the tall woman at his side. When she touched his arm he turned to the touch.

"I'm going," she said. "I'll get coffee ready and blankets."

"I'll stay," he said, "lest I am wanted." They nodded, suddenly close in a common tragedy.

He came back from the funeral services the next day, sorrowful to his own door. This time there had been five men to be buried together. He had taken care of the dead while the living had been sent to Allis, and they had not met again.

"There's somebody waitin' for you in the livin' room," Mrs. Hardman said when he opened the front door of the manse.

"Who is it?" he said.

"A Jap," she said briefly.

A Japanese! He had not known there was one in Beechey. He went quickly into the room. There indeed was a Japanese, a small quivering man in a rusty black suit, his hair too long and in his thin little hands a shapeless black hat. Behind his thick spectacles his eyes were terrified, though he opened his mouth in a wide smile.

"Please sit down," Briony said in Japanese.

The man sat down on the edge of a chair, the hat still in his hands, still with the fixed smile on his face.

"What can I do for you?" Briony asked. He knew that the smile meant fear.

The man pointed with a shaking forefinger to the golden bowl on the mantelpiece. "You got that—in Japan?" he asked in a high little voice like a child's.

"My friends there gave it to me," Briony replied.

"Japanese friends?" the little man asked.

"I had many Japanese friends," Briony said. "I lived there a long time."

The man's face had been tensely composed but now he stared at Briony, blinked once or twice, and then without any warning he put his hand over his face and began to weep aloud, gasping in small high sobs. Briony, seated opposite him, looked down to the hearth rug and waited. He knew of old this kind of thing in a Japanese, the smile, the seeming composure, the sudden break. So Ake had wept in those last days. But he had seen Mr. Kato, too, beside the deathbed of his only son smile and turn away calmly. They had gone out-side into the garden and Mr. Kato had called his attention to a very fine peony coming into bloom. Then while they had stood looking at it, Mr. Kato had put his hand to his face and had begun to weep aloud, like this.

So now Briony waited but when the gasping sobs grew hysterical he began to talk quietly.

"You are very disturbed, I know, over the outbreak of this war. So am I. Our countries have long been friends, after their fashion—until now."

"I am—in America long time," the little man choked.

"Good," Briony said. "Then you have nothing to fear."

But the little man shook his head. "Citizen—don't matter much," he said. He was getting the better now of his sobs. He wiped his eyes carefully on the cuff of his faded shirt sleeve, which was very clean. "They don't like Japanese. My shop—no more people."

"What is your shop?" Briony asked.

"Sukiyaki," the little man said. "Yis, today, every day, nobody come. On street, small boy say I poison people. Me, Hasu! I long time New York, so my wife sick, I come here for her fresh air from sea now three—four years. I never see Jopon since very young. My wife Jopon. Can't talk American. So—" He drew in his breath. "We hear you live Jopon and today she say, 'tell him,' that is, you."

The little man leaned forward, the tears glistening on his face. "What to do, sir?" he asked softly.

Briony shook his head. "I don't know," he said. He sat thinking a moment, aware of the eager myopic black eyes on his face. "It is strange," he said slowly, "a few months ago, it was I in Japan, asking what to do. Now it is you, here, asking the same question."

The little man burst out at him, "Until now, so nice! Everybody this side they like me—now, one day, they don't like me!"

"I know how it is," Briony said.

He looked out of the window and saw the small yard tangled with weeds. "If your business is not worth keeping open," he said, "you may come and make a garden for me. I'd like to show the people in Beechey what a Japanese can do with some trees and a piece of weedy ground."

The little man's lips quivered again. He dropped his hat and picked it up. "Thank you," he said, "I thank you very much, sir. You save our lifes."

He rose and bowed himself away, and Briony bowed and

followed him to the door and closed it behind him. In the back hall Mrs. Hardman was sweeping.

"Mrs. Hardman," he said gravely. "Will it upset you if Mr. Hasu works on the yard?"

"Nothin' upsets me," she said shortly, "not at my time of life."

"Good," he said, and went back to his study.

Then he heard her call and he paused at the door.

"Though I'm not the whole of Beechey," she said.

"I understand that," he said and closed the door behind him.

"But for such a miserable creature!" Allis was saying impetuously. Her house was empty again. The sailors she had fed and cared for were gone, and she had written a little note to tell him so. "And you might come to tea," she had added. So he had come, at once, the same day. Her beautiful hands moved with decision among the Spode teacups. "Where's your sense of proportion, Jim? One wretched Japanese! I never liked them."

He had been telling Allis that he had had to bring Hasu indoors today because boys, passing, had thrown stones at him in the yard.

"Hasu is certainly not the best of his people," he admitted to Allis with his faint smile. "Though his wife is nice and he has a charming little daughter."

"Don't make me like them," she said promptly. "I don't want to be tolerant or good or pleasant or human or any of those Christian things. When I think of that burning ship I want to hate the enemy and enjoy it, Jim." Her blue eyes glittered.

He laughed suddenly. She was so little changed! "I don't want you to be a Christian," he said, "in fact, I don't believe you could be, Allis."

"None of my friends would know me if I were," she retorted, "and I prefer to keep my friends."

"Then you must allow me in the same spirit to keep poor Hasu," he said. "It is a small act of gratitude to Japan for much friendship shown me in the past." And then he told her about the golden bowl.

"Someday when you're not looking," she said, "I am going to smash it into little bits."

"You wouldn't!" he cried. But he was not sure.

She shook her head. "Somebody must break it," she declared, "or you'll never be free of Japan. They've put some heathen magic into that bowl."

He looked at her helplessly. Something in him she would never understand so long as they lived and however close they drew together. He was now beginning to admit the possibility of their drawing very close, but he would not allow himself to love her. For love meant marriage, and marriage was impossible. He could take no dead man's fortune as part of his marriage. He wondered, too sensitive, if that was why she had so immediately told him about that wicked will? Did she want him to know, from the first moment they met again, that marriage was impossible? Then he would never by any word betray to her a sign of love.

"You're handsomer than ever, Jim," she said suddenly.

"You are more beautiful than ever," he replied gravely.

And then he was troubled. What folly made him suddenly want to put into words the disturbance he felt because—because he saw her white hands over the teacups, and because they were alone in the quiet, noble room, and because her eyes were so clear and so blue, and he was lonely?

He went back to the manse very soon and in the living room he took the golden bowl from the mantelpiece. It felt smooth and cold to the touch. He thought of what she had said about breaking it. It could be easily broken, indeed. If it should fall now from his hands, by an accident, upon the hearthstone, it would be shattered beyond repair.

"Oh, it's you!" Mrs. Hardman said suddenly at the door.

He jumped and clutched the bowl. "I nearly dropped it!" he cried.

"It gives me conniptions, that thing," Mrs. Hardman said, "every time I dust it, it's that smooth in my hands."

He set it back on the mantel and felt his forehead cold with sweat.

"Never break that bowl, Mrs. Hardman," he said gravely.

But behind his back Mrs. Hardman was already gone and he was speaking only to himself.

"A letter that concerns you, Jim," Allis said. She had ridden to the door of the manse, and now she sat reining her horse back from the threshold. Hasu, his knees carefully padded with bits of rags, stared at her as he pulled weeds. His small daughter stood with her feet far apart and let her solemn black eyes follow up the immense height of the horse's legs.

Briony had opened the door himself, seeing Allis from the window of the living room where he worked when Hasu was in the front yard. He had to stand guard always now for Hasu when the schoolchildren were passing. But this was the middle of the morning and the street was quiet. Setsu came to his side and took his finger.

"Come in, Allis," he said, admiring her in the clear morning light.

She gave him a look suddenly shy and young. Then she slipped from her horse and they went into the manse, the little Japanese child still clinging to his finger. He led her into the living room, and her eyes went straight to the mantelpiece. The bowl was there, but she did not speak of it.

"Sit down," he said, and sat down himself. Against his knee the fat little Japanese child leaned, barefooted and wearing nothing but her small red cotton rompers.

Allis sat down. "That baby acts as though you were her father," she said. She smiled without mirth. It was not too foreign to him to have a Japanese child! "Why didn't you marry a Japanese woman, Jim? You really like them better than you do us."

"It is not true that I like the Japanese better than my own people," he said sternly. "I do not think of peoples. I think of human beings. They are everywhere."

"Preacher!" she said, laughing, and then with pretended carelessness she drew a folded sheet from her pocket. "Here's the letter," she said, and tossed it to him. The Japanese baby laughed as he caught it.

"Funny!" she remarked in a hearty little voice.

He rumpled her straight fringe of black hair and opened the letter that was addressed to Allis.

"Dear Allis," it said, "It seems to me your preacher is the ideal man for our job. Why not send him along? He ought to know the Japs. Twenty years, my God!" The name at the end was Hal Schwartz.

"What do you want me to do?" Briony asked. The handwriting was bold and hard on heavy linenlike paper. "I see you must have written the letter to which this is only the answer."

Allis leaned forward. "Jim, I wrote to Hal Schwartz that you were a big man in a little place. You're being wasted here, Jim. Beechey—you, speaking Japanese and reading Japanese, and preaching here to a handful of fishermen and a couple of garagemen and a grocer!"

"Who is Hal Schwartz?" he asked.

She looked away. "A friend of mine—in a way," she said.

"But that's not so important as his being in charge of propaganda at that office."

"I don't like propaganda," Briony said, frowning. "The people in Japan were always being fed it—a lot of lies, I call it."

"Jim, it's wartime!" Allis cried.

The little Japanese child watching that vivid face of hers put her hand into Briony's and he closed his hand over it. Allis was scarcely aware that she saw it, but he knew she did, she leaned forward and spoke with a new passion.

"Jim, people are beginning to say you are pro-Japanese! Everybody knows you have moved this family here. Jim, it's dangerous. If you help Hal Schwartz, everybody will have to stop talking."

Briony did not let go of the small brown hand.

She went on, wishing she could put the child out of the room.

"Jim, this is a chance to do something wonderful for the war. You can speak to millions of people—over the radio."

"What would I say, Allis?"

She did not answer for the briefest moment. There was such innocence in his dark eyes, such goodness in his calm face, that she could not speak. Instead she rose, half-impatient with his goodness now, as she had been when they were young. If he had not been so good they would never have parted.

"Why don't you go and talk to Hal Schwartz yourself?" she said. "You can be quite frank with him. Besides, it's not for me. You ought to as an American."

She was not sure that she had touched him at any point and she wanted to touch him. She wanted for curiously mixed reasons to persuade him and save him and make him her own. There was that bowl—shining on the mantelpiece.

She did want to smash it. As long as he loved Japan he would not love her. And now suddenly she knew she wanted him to love her. She rose and went to him impulsively and put her hand on his shoulder and stood looking down at him.

"Go," she said, her blue eyes warm upon his upturned face. "Go for my sake, Jim. I want you to be—safe."

She touched his cheek with her soft palm. "Promise me!" she said.

He dropped the child's hand and seized her wrists, putting both her hands to his cheeks. She had touched him at last. She saw a sudden heat in his dark eyes.

"I will," he said, "I will—if you want me to!"

She smiled deeply into his eyes. The little child, staring at them, suddenly ran out of the room. They were alone.

"Allis!" he gasped.

"Hush!" she whispered. She pulled her soft hands away and before he could gather his senses she was gone.

"Dr. Briony?"

"Yes," James Briony said.

He met calmly a pair of sharp round gray eyes that shot beams of cold light at him across a big desk in an office in New York. Behind the desk was a huge window, full of sky-scrapers.

"Allis Earle tells me you are just the man for us," said Hal Schwartz.

Briony smiled at this without answering. Around him the hum of a new organization had an undertone of frenzy, like bees uncertain of their hive. The thick-set man across the desk looked harried and determined and angry.

"We have the devil of a job on our hands," he said in his harsh, abrupt voice. "This war has to be fought and the people aren't ready to fight it. We went in too late, as usual. Now we have to get the people into the frame of mind that will make them hate the Japs. You'd think Pearl Harbor would do it, but it hasn't."

Briony did not break his silence. He continued to gaze steadily at the hard face across the desk. It was, he decided, a New York kind of face. It was impossible to tell what had been this man's forebears.

"These people," Schwartz said, "can't see any farther than their little towns and cities. Well, they'd better, or they'll find themselves out in the cold. I tell you, we've got to win this war, and there's only one way to win it. You've got to hate these Japs and hate 'em hard enough to kill 'em."

Briony lifted his big thin hand and covered his mouth instinctively to hide its change. His mind flew back to his church in Japan and the quiet patient faces looking toward him. "How do you propose to arouse this hatred?" he asked.

"Why, simply tell 'em about the Japs," Schwartz said contemptuously. "Tell 'em how mean and yellow they are—a treacherous lot!"

"But how would one do this?" Briony inquired.

Schwartz leaned back. "That's what I wanted you to come here for," he said. "You've lived in Japan for twenty years, you must've seen them at their worst. Well, I want you to think of the worst and tell it to the country—I'll get you radio time and you can talk to millions."

Briony locked his hands together tightly, his elbows on the arms of his chair. Those locked hands were a symbolic barrier to keep his anger from bursting out of his bosom. "The necessity is not to hate the people of Japan," he said at last. "It is to be sure that what we fight for is the right."

Schwartz reached for a cigarette from a heavy silver box on his desk. "A preacher, aren't you?"

"Think of me as a man," Briony said.

"You've been away from America a long time," Schwartz retorted.

"I was born here, an American," Briony replied.

He rose as he spoke and stood, very tall, looking down at the man behind the desk. "I've been here a long time," he repeated, "my grandfather and my great-grandfather were here. His father fought in the Revolutionary War. My grandfather fought for the freedom of slaves."

Schwartz banged his hand on his desk. "I'm too busy to bother if you don't want to do it," he said sharply. "But I feel like reporting you, Briony."

"Where?" Briony was about to ask and did not. It did not matter. He had taken his stand. He bowed slightly and left the room. Outside in the hall he stood waiting for the elevator, seeing none of the people around him. They glanced at him because he was so tall, because he carried his head high and looked somehow foreign in his bearing. But he saw none of them. He was thinking of Allis. He would have to tell her he could not do what had been asked of him. He would have to tell her so that she would understand. He was not at all sure that he could.

"You see how impossible it was, Allis," he said. He was very tired but he had come straight from the station to her house. The house seemed heaven to him tonight in its quiet and orderly beauty. The great trees stood about it in the moonlight like sentinels. She herself was quieter than usual, gentle as though with the night. He wanted to pour himself out to her.

"How could I teach hatred against people who have been good to me for twenty years?"

"Perhaps the trouble is that you cannot teach hatred against anyone," she said. She leaned back in the deep chair in which she sat. The light was low and the wide doors were open before them, and almost side by side with only a small table between them, they sat facing the garden under the moon.

"Yes, perhaps that is my trouble," he said quietly. He thought to himself that he had never hated anyone in his life. It was hard to begin now.

"And yet," she said, "how can men be asked to kill those whom they do not hate?"

"I do not ask it," he replied.

Across their difference she was reaching toward him, longing for him. The three days since she had seen him were restless with her uncertainty. Yes, she knew she loved him. Then the certainty had smitten her again like a sword this very night as she saw him coming up the steps to her house less than an hour ago. He had come straight to her and she was waiting for him.

"How shall we win this war?" she asked.

"Hate never wins anything," he replied. "What it wins it will lose again."

"Then you won't do it?" she asked.

"Certainly I will not," he replied.

He looked suddenly remote as he spoke and she had a moment's terror. What if he could never love her?

"We are back where we were," she said.

He looked at her, not comprehending. "I mean, where we were twenty-one years ago," she said, "when you would not give up—and I would not—"

He cried out at her. "But, Allis, you always ask the same thing of me—my own conscience!"

"You are so little changed," she agreed.

But she said to herself that she was ready to give up to him, to yield at last and accept him as he was. What did anything matter except that he had come back?

Then he said slowly, "I suppose that we must face the

truth—I would not have come back from Japan had I not been compelled to it by this war."

She rose quickly. "You really haven't come back," she said. "I am very tired—I think perhaps you had better go." She put out her hand quickly and touched his. "Goodbye." She left him and he heard her mount the stairs and then after a moment of standing there, silent and listening, he went away. They were far apart indeed.

"I dare not love her," he thought as he walked home.

He was very tired indeed. The sound of the sea was a solemn roar in the black night. There were no lights anywhere now along the shore, lest enemy submarines be guided by them to attack the ships that however closely they crept along the shore still went in danger.

But Hasu had kept the night light burning in the hall of the manse and when he heard the door open he came in from the kitchen. He had been asleep and his hair stood up in straight spikes.

"You back?" he inquired.

"Yes, I am back," Briony said. He really did not like Hasu. He had none of the grace of a Japanese in Japan. He was a common little man, timid and rude together. Briony would have been glad to have him gone, and yet to put him out now would be too cruel. At this moment he liked him less than ever. "Thank you for waiting," he said to Hasu.

"That's nothing," Hasu said. "There is supper Mrs. Hardman left in the kitchen. Want me to get it?"

"No, thanks, I'll not eat tonight," Briony said. He went into his study and shut the door and fell upon his knees. This time it was harder than it had been twenty-one years ago. He could not sail upon a ship and leave her far away. He had to stay here, in his own country, and hers—and not yield up his soul. "I will not teach hatred," he said, sternly to himself upon his knees.

But he went on thinking. His own country—in some way could he tell people what he himself believed? They were being told they had to hate their enemies. His mind recalled swiftly the faces he knew best—Mr. and Mrs. Capey and Job Hendry and Captain Jackson and all the fishermen whose names he had learned carefully, and their wives and their children. He had so long been used to Japanese names that for a while the American names had slipped from him. But he knew them now, Bascom and Standwick and Landis and Brown, Avery and Prescott and Deems and Lester—faces came to his call, good faces, less disciplined than the faces he knew in Japan, more hearty, more full of temper, less calm, but no more disposed to hatred.

"If I could get them to see each other for what they are," he thought, "if I could get Ake and Mr. Kato to know what these people are and the Ayama family to know the Bascoms, for instance! They are really so much alike."

He fell into the musing thought out of which always came his swiftest action. Large shapes began to grow in his mind. What if he could simply begin to explain people to each other? For instance, if he could say to Mr. Kato, "The people here in America do not hate you. They want to help free you from the things which you yourself consider hateful. We Americans, for example, Mr. Kato, do not believe in putting people into prison for what they think."

Yes, he and Mr. Kato had spent many mornings discussing the evil of imprisoning young men and women as they were imprisoned in Japan for thinking what was called "dangerous thoughts." Actually these were only such thoughts as people in America took as a matter of course.

"I would like to tell Mr. Kato that here in America we believe in these dangerous thoughts—we believe in people thinking as they feel it is right to think." He was still on his knees—was not God speaking to him?

But how could he reach Mr. Kato? He remembered suddenly what Hal Schwartz had said—"millions over the radio."
Of course—Mr. Kato had a radio. Maybe it had been taken
away from him, but he doubted it. Mr. Kato was very re-
sourceful. He would hide that little shortwave radio set—
perhaps in the small ancestral shrine in the garden. No one
would think of looking in such a place. But Mr. Kato did not
mind sacrilege—he was very modern. He had made the shortwave set himself, with old-fashioned earphones, so that no
one else could use it.

"But how could I get to Mr. Kato from here," he asked
God at this moment.

He never doubted that of course it was God who told him
to write to the President in Washington and tell him about
the many men in Japan who were like Mr. Kato. He must ask
the President that he be allowed to speak direct to the Japanese, and tell them what the people in America really were
like.

In the large simplicity of his being James Briony rose from
his knees, perfectly sure of his duty. He took from his desk
envelope and paper and in his clear handwriting, which
looked like old English print, he addressed a letter to the
President of the United States asking that he be allowed to
speak to the people of Japan about being free to think, to
talk, as the people in America were free. "I believe God
brought me back for this," he told the President.

He finished the letter, signing it as he would have to a
friend, "Yours faithfully," and he sealed it in the envelope
and stamped and addressed it. Then he took it himself to the
mailbox at the corner of the street. It did not occur to him
that he would not get an answer. God, of course, would also
direct the President.

He went back into the manse and up to his room. He felt

relieved and clear again. When he was in bed he fell instantly asleep as a child does who has been made secure.

In the vestry of his church the next Sunday Briony stood in the same calm and faced the seven men who sat there waiting for him after church. No answer had come to his letter, but tomorrow it would come. Meanwhile he was not in the least disturbed by a notice that the vestrymen wished to talk with him today after church. He had not taken off his robes and now he wrapped them about him as he sat down.

"Mr. Hendry you called this as an extraordinary meeting?" he said pleasantly. "I am at your service."

He was usually very tired after his sermon but this morning the strength of his own emotion had not left him. He had begun his work. To a surprised congregation he had spoken with all his heart of man's duty to love his fellow man and not to hate him. Across the sea the enemy was bombing helpless American boys hiding in ditches. The mother of one of those boys broke into sobs in the middle of his sermon and her husband had risen and together they had left the church. A murmur had gone over the congregation, but he had silenced it with his own ringing voice: "And still I say that under God's command we may hate no man, whatever evil he does to us. Evil only we may hate."

Though he did not know it, he had put into what he said all the power of his own beauty, all the magic of his voice. He spoke to his people of what seemed right to him, and he spoke the more clearly because Allis was not there. He had seen the moment that he entered the church that she was not there. He had not heard from her nor had he sought her. Now he knew without asking what this little group of stolid good men wanted of him but he was not disturbed.

"We come here to say what we think," Job Hendry said slowly. Job Hendry was the grocer. "We been thinkin' it a long time, but we haven't felt free to speak until now. Some didn't want we should."

"Yes?" Briony leaned forward in the tall ecclesiastical chair and smiled. He had friends in his congregation. "Who are my friends?" Briony asked.

The men looked at each other and coughed. Job spoke again. "To tell the truth, it's been Miss Earle. Of course the session don't listen to a woman. But, after all, the Earle family done a good deal for the town. The old man built the liberry."

"I see!" Briony said. Allis? His heart softened. "But I don't want anyone to keep you from your duty," he said. "Tell me what you are thinking."

"We don't think you ought to keep that Jap in the manse," Job said bluntly. The men sat like statues. Since Job had been elected to speak, no one else would speak. "The manse," Job said ponderously, "belongs to the church. The church don't want that there should be enemies in the manse."

"They are only in the garage," Briony said, his dark eyes glinting with mirth. These little men—these good little men! He suddenly remembered a Mr. Hakimoto, with whom once he had argued that one should not despise a tribesman from the northern islands of Japan.

"Same thing," one of the six statues said suddenly. "On the church grounds, that is."

The others stared at him severely and he retreated into silence.

"Shall I turn that little family out into the street?" Briony inquired. "You know they have no way to make a living. They cannot help the war any more than you and I can."

Seven pairs of eyes stared at him. He could see their brains struggling with this matter of right and wrong.

"Will you let me think for a few days what I should do?" he asked gently. "Let me talk with Hasu and see what his resources are."

The seven looked at each other. A voice spoke out of uncertainty. "Well, all right, but we still think he ought to get out."

"I am glad you have told me what you think," he said courteously.

He waited alone for a few moments after they had gone. Then he took off his surplice and hung it in a closet and went home. On the lawn of the manse Setsu had made a small square garden of pebbles. He stepped across it carefully. Not for anything would he have disturbed the little world in which Setsu lived.

It was evening before he spoke to Hasu. He waited until Mrs. Hardman had gone to bed and the house was silent. Out in the garage Hasu's wife had gone to bed and Setsu, too, was asleep. But he had told Hasu to come into the study at ten o'clock. He sat reading and waiting for the scratch on the door which was Hasu's knock. In Japan he would have coughed.

"Come in," he said when he heard it and Hasu came in, wearing a clean shirt and no coat. In Japan he would not have thought of coming in without his coat.

"Sit down," Briony said. Hasu sat down unsmiling.

Briony began to speak simply and clearly, having planned what he would say. "Hasu, you know this is not my house and the garage is not my garage. It belongs to the people of the church. Now they feel that because you are a Japanese you should not stay here. They want you to go away."

Hasu's face paled. "Where to go?" His voice came out of his throat huskily and he coughed to clear it.

"That is what I wish to ask," Briony said kindly. "Have you anyone?"

"Nobody," Hasu said. "Nobody." He looked about the book-lined room. "These all your books?"

Only someone who had lived twenty years in Japan could understand that Hasu asked the question not out of interest but acute anxiety, not about the books, but about what Briony had said.

"Yes, they are mine," Briony said gently. "Then, Hasu, if you have nowhere to go, you shall stay here. But you are staying here only because I am promising the people that you are honest. That is, whatever you now do that is wrong it will be my fault. I am responsible for you."

He saw a flicker of fear in Hasu's eyes as he gazed steadily at the man. Then Hasu laughed. "Sure," he said, "sure, Doctor Briony. I'm very honest man."

He looked restlessly about the room and rose and twisted his hands together into a tight knot. "Thanking you," he said suddenly.

"Do you understand what I have said, Hasu?" Briony asked.

"Yis, understand all right," Hasu said.

"Then good night, Hasu."

"Good night, Dr. Briony, sir."

He waited while Hasu went out. The door shut. He could hear no sound of footsteps. But that was because Hasu wore soft cloth slippers that his wife made.

Briony stood, listening. He had made himself responsible for a Japanese he really did not know. What if Hasu were not trustworthy? Then he rebuked himself. "I am growing like everyone else in this war," he thought. "I am imagining that because a man is Japanese he must be an enemy. How evil war is—we are all poisoned by it."

He remembered his clean little house at the foot of Fuji and how at night its unpainted wooden beams had smelled of sweet pine. Nostalgia stirred him. That Japan was still there.

He went into the living room across the hall. There the golden bowl was upon the mantelpiece. He took it in his hands and held it away from him, gazing at it.

"I am going to keep it in my study," he thought. "I want to live with it."

No, Hasu might be a common little man but he was not necessarily a villain. He took the bowl under his arm and went back to his study and set it upon the mantelpiece. Then he cleared everything away, so that it stood there alone. Such was its beauty, he thought, that nothing should be near it. He sat down and lit his pipe and in quiet he let his mind remember, and in remembering he thought of Allis. How good of her, while she disapproved him, that she had asked the session not to speak to him of Hasu! The temptation to tell her so grew in him and at last he yielded to it. He was hungry for the excuse to hear her speak. He had not seen her since that night. But he had thought perhaps when the letter came he would tell her. Yet why had he to wait? He took up the telephone and was rewarded by her voice, low and clear.

"Yes?"

"Allis, it is I—have I disturbed you?"

"No, of course not, Jim."

"I wanted only to thank you, Allis, for holding back my good men of the vestry."

"I? Oh, that was nothing. I only laughed at them a little—and told them to wait."

"They listened to your laughter, then." He hesitated, wanting to hear her voice go on. Then he was surprised by her sudden cry. "Jim!"

"Yes—what is it?"

"Jim, I am in my room, in bed. My south window faces the manse. Jim, there is a light flashing off and on in your little attic window—"

"Allis—there can't be!"

"Yes, Jim, there it goes again—one, two, three—"

He dropped the receiver and sped away into the hall and up the stairs three at a time and reached the attic door and burst it open. He switched on the light. No one was there. He searched and still found no one. Then he saw something flung into a corner. It was one of Hasu's cloth shoes, kicked off as if in haste. He looked again and found its mate. He leaned out of the window. The roof went steeply down into a mass of old lilacs. He could see nothing. It was too dark.

He hurried downstairs again and out to the garage and pounded the door. No one came and he pounded again. Then Hasu came to the door blinking, his hair on end. He was in his pajamas.

"Hasu, here are your shoes," Briony said sternly.

The Japanese drew in his breath. "So!" he breathed. "I left them in the attic."

"Why were you in the attic?" Briony demanded.

"Today I clean," Hasu said. "Mrs. Hardman, she say the dust make her cough. She say, 'Hasu, you go.'"

"But you had these shoes on when you came to my study!"

Hasu smiled suddenly and shook his head. "No, anothers," he said. "I forget these in attic today so I put on some more tonight." He turned and trotted away and in a moment was back, bringing a pair exactly like the ones Briony had found.

Briony stared down at the little man, searching for the soul in those narrow black eyes. But whatever the soul was, it was well hid. Hasu gazed back, blinking once or twice.

"Well, good night, Hasu," Briony said abruptly.

"Good night, Dr. Briony, sir," Hasu said and closed the door.

In the study he took up the receiver again. "Allis?"

"Waiting," her voice said, "ages."

"I can't find a thing—Hasu's shoes, but it seems Mrs. Hardman asked him to clean the attic today and he forgot them there. I remember that he always takes them off whenever he mops a floor. He never wears socks."

"Certainly I saw the light, Jim," she said.

"I don't doubt it," he said. "I'll keep watching."

"Good night, Jim."

"Good night—dear." The word came of itself from his lips. He waited, horrified. What had he said? His heart had leaped from his lips. There was silence, then he heard her voice very faint. "Good night—" He waited but there was nothing more.

That night hours later he awoke, uneasy. Then he remembered suddenly how Allis had cried out. Allis was not one to imagine things. What she had seen had been there. He rose and taking a flashlight went up to the attic again and searched in it thoroughly. It was almost empty, as attics are in most manses, and was not hard to search. He was about to give up, finding nothing, until he saw a door opening under the eaves, a door too small to enter except for his head and shoulders. But he opened it, and circled his flashlight into it. There he saw against the inner wall a large lantern, new and polished. He drew it toward him and examined it. It was full of oil and the wick was trimmed.

His heart stopped and then began to beat again hard. It was a lantern he had bought for the garage, because the electricity was not connected when Hasu first came. What should he do with it? For a moment he thought of taking it to Hasu at once and demanding to know why it was here. He thought a moment and put it back exactly where he found it.

Tomorrow morning he would ask Mrs. Hardman about it.

But the next morning he forgot everything. For beside his plate in the morning's mail was a heavy white envelope. He recognized it at once. It was the answer to his letter. He tore it open quickly. Yes, there it was, a simple answer, asking him to come to Washington and tell them what he could do.

He folded the letter reverently. So God moved through ways that were great and small! Once when he had been in Japan he had been distressed because of the conditions in a certain part of the city near which he lived and he had written direct to the Emperor, telling no one. There had been no answer in a letter, but soon after that the district had been greatly improved, old houses torn down and clean new ones put up for the poor.

"Mrs. Hardman," he said, "I am going away. I shall be back tomorrow night." He pondered a moment as to whether he would tell anyone where he was going and decided he would not. No, he would not tell even Allis. He had always worked in secret with God. If he told people they were inclined to laugh at him and say that what he had undertaken was impossible. Even Allis, perhaps, would laugh, and that of all laughter he could not endure. For of course nothing was impossible.

Mrs. Hardman brought in his egg and then, seeing her, he again remembered last night. It seemed not important now, but still he would ask.

"Mrs. Hardman, did you tell Hasu to clean the attic yesterday?"

Mrs. Hardman looked at him apologetically. "I did," she said. "I know he's for the yard, but I had my asthma yesterday somethin' awful. I didn't think you'd mind."

"I don't," he said. "Did he do a good job?"

"I told him to," she said, sharply. "He said the light wasn't too good and I told him to take that big lantern you bought and carry it around with him."

He drank his coffee, smiling at himself. So he had lost a night's sleep over nothing at all! He looked out of the window and his eyes fell on Hasu, on his knees pulling weeds.

Suddenly the matter of a light in an attic window seemed nothing. He had work to do.

He went to Washington, a lonely figure, known only, he thought, to God, and conspicuous only because he was so tall and his garments were old-fashioned in their cut and slightly threadbare. It had not occurred to him to buy new clothes. In Washington he was lost two or three times until someone pointed out the White House and there he went, presenting his letter for a passport. Guards escorted him through a vast hall and then into a room where a gray-haired man sat, not the President, he saw at once, but someone whom doubtless God had prepared.

"Sit down, please," the man said. He was not in the least like Hal Schwartz, and in a few minutes James Briony was speaking very simply of the idea that had come to him and that now appeared to be his duty. The gray-haired man listened. He did not tell his name and Briony did not ask it. Names did not matter when there was God's work to be done.

"A very interesting idea," the man said. "We are disposed to try it, Dr. Briony. I wonder if you could go to this address—in New York"—he wrote something down on a sheet of paper—"and simply speak once or twice a week, as often as you can, as often as you feel ready to speak."

"You mean—my voice will be heard in Japan?"

"We hope so," the man said smiling.

There was little to be said after that. So easily did God work! He took up his somewhat rusty hat and walked down the great hall again. Thus had Christ performed his miracles, by a word, a movement of his hand. So would this miracle be performed in that name. He, James Briony, a man of no importance, would speak of an important thing, and Mr. Kato in Japan, and all the Mr. Katos listening, would hear him and understand why this war was being fought. They would understand that Americans did not hate them and that they fought for freedom for everybody. He breathed a great sigh. Ever since the war had broken out between the two countries he had been wanting to explain to Japan why it had to be fought. Now he could do it. He took two wrong turns and then, set right by a stranger, he arrived at the station and took a day coach for home. He was already planning his first sermon to Japan.

"Hasu is gone," Mrs. Hardman said. She was waiting for him at the front door.

"Gone!" he cried.

"Police," she said, "came and took him at five minutes past eleven." Her rather light gray eyes flickered as he looked at her.

"What did they say?" he inquired, full of horror.

"Didn't say nothin'—just ast for you and then took him along."

She went back to the kitchen and he hurried out of the house to the garage. The door was shut and he pushed it open. Inside Mrs. Hasu sat, holding Setsu in her arms. Her small eyes were red and Setsu was piteous with weeping.

He said in Japanese, "What has happened, Hasu-san?"

Her soft, shapeless face quivered. "They have taken him," she said. "Where have they taken him, sir?"

Setsu began to cry again, soundlessly.

"I don't know," he said. "Don't grieve. I shall go and find him." How helpless were these in time of war! So helpless had he been in Japan. "Come, Setsu, come out and play." But the little child clung to her mother and there was nothing that he could do at last but to go away and leave them, and this he did, closing the door behind him.

He told Mrs. Hardman that he would not eat, and getting

into his old car again he drove to the police station. He went in and found a burly man sitting behind his desk.

"I have come to see about my hired man, Hasu Takimoto," he said.

"He's locked up," the man said gruffly.

"May I ask on what charge?" Briony asked.

"On suspicion," the man said.

"Is that all you will tell me?" Briony asked.

"That's all," the man said.

Briony hesitated. "Can I see him?"

"No," the man said. He glared at Briony. Then he spoke very slowly. "And let me tell you, I don't like what I hear about you around here, either."

Briony looked at him without a change of his usual amiable calm.

"What do you hear?" he asked pleasantly.

"Never you mind," the man growled.

An immense distaste for the man's thick red jowls filled Briony's slender body. He felt disgust run through his veins. He turned away. "Very well, I won't mind," he said.

He was determined to be calm, but calm was impossible when he thought of that ruthless and lowering red face. How would he explain this sort of thing to Mr. Kato? He suddenly felt more terrified than he had ever felt in his life. This was the sort of thing that made people in Japan afraid. Then he put his terror aside. "Why should I be afraid?" he thought. "This isn't Japan—it's my own country."

But as he turned in at his own lane three policemen stepped suddenly from the bushes and stopped his car. He opened the door and peered out at them. They came nearer.

"James Briony, you are under arrest," one of them said.

His head went dizzy and for a moment he thought he would faint. Then he turned off the engine of his car and stepped out.

"Why am I arrested?" he demanded.

"On suspicion," the man said.

"What suspicion?" he demanded.

"You'll find out," the man answered. "Will you come along or shall we—"

"Certainly I will come," he replied. "But I will put my car in the garage, if you please." He got back into the car, and the man stepped in with him. In silence they drove the few hundred yards to the manse and Briony ran his car into the lane and locked it. At the door of the garage Mrs. Hasu and Setsu watched him with terrified eyes. But they did not speak.

"Now," Briony said, "if you please."

In silence he stepped into the side car of a motorcycle. They went swiftly through the darkness to the police station. The station house was empty. But the men took him through it to the jail behind it.

"Here's your hotel," one of them said, and laughed—a very young man he was, Briony saw by the hard electric light that poured down everywhere from ceiling lights. He followed them down a corridor, there was the clank of a key and a metal door grated. He found himself in a small bare room whose furniture was a cot and a stool and a washstand. The door locked on him again. He stood gazing about him, and suddenly he smiled grimly to himself.

"My own country!" he murmured. Down the long corridor the footsteps of the departing men sounded in hollow echoes.

How would he ever talk to Mr. Kato now?

Sometime in the night—he could not tell what time because the cell lights were suddenly turned off and there was only the corridor light shining through the bars of the door—he got up and went to the small barred window. He stared out into the night. It was perhaps midnight or a little later, judging by the old moon now waning. By climbing on the cot he could see, with his unusual height, a fair distance. The land began to shape in his mind. There was the church steeple, and beside it would be the manse. He stared at the gray darkness, and suddenly he saw a light. It shone on and off three times. Then there were perhaps five minutes of darkness and twice more it flashed. He stared, forgetting where he was. The attic window, he thought in agitation! But what on earth —who—he watched for another hour but there was no more light.

He lay the rest of the night sleepless. But Hasu was in jail, too. Then who was there in the attic? Could it be Mrs. Hasu? That soft and childish creature—was she carrying on treachery for Hasu's sake? He could not imagine it and yet so much that he could not imagine today had happened.

And then as he thought of the lights flashing off and on from his own attic, he heard the deep roar of an explosion out to sea.

He shouted at the top of his strength, and he ran to the door and beat upon it with his fists. But no one heard.

The chief of police the next morning was irritable and ready to be angry—Briony saw this the moment he was led into the room between two guards. He had been called suddenly out of his belated sleep.

The man behind the desk looked up as he came in and then deliberately kept him waiting three minutes, four minutes, five minutes. It was the sort of thing that Mr. Kato used to tell him about, Briony thought, and smiled slightly. Obviously the big man was enjoying his importance. Briony stood waiting, detached and seemingly patient until suddenly the man threw down the stubby pencil he had been using and shouted at him.

"You're under suspicion!"

Briony stopped smiling. "I should think I would be," he said gravely. "Those lights flashing off and on in my own attic last night—"

"What's that?" the man roared. "Why, there was a ship sunk last night, off the cape!"

"I heard the explosion," Briony said, "and I feared that was what it was. But what could I do? I was locked in a cell, and I shouted and I shook the door. But no one came."

"Who could have been in that attic?" the man demanded.

"I don't know," Briony replied. "Hasu is in jail, too. Of course it might be his wife. I thought of that—though I don't believe she's the guilty—"

"You're guilty unless you prove not guilty these days," the man declared. He looked at Briony with sudden shrewdness. His voice changed into a gimlet, hard and cold and screwing. "What are you up to, Briony? You're playing the innocent."

Briony stared down at him, in surprise. "But I am innocent." He hesitated a moment and then said honestly, "Of course I can see how things look—the lights in the attic, and then I suppose—my ideas—are what you would call 'dangerous thoughts.' "

The man's mouth sneered at him. "You have a record against you, Briony. It seems you refused to do propaganda for the war."

"No," Briony murmured. He tried not to look at the man's swelling red neck. "Only not to do propaganda for hate—"

"You gotta hate 'em if you want to fight 'em—" the man growled.

"Not me," Briony said steadfastly.

"You're one of these damned conscientious objectors!" the man sneered.

Briony lost his temper suddenly, an Irish temper at bottom that had been only superficially gentle through years of peace. Yet once in Japan he had almost hit a man like this one, before whom an innocent peasant cringed. Well, he would not cringe! He leaned forward and his long right arm shot out. There was a leathery thud and the chief of police cringed in his chair.

"I beg your pardon!" Briony said horrified.

"Take him away!" the man roared, holding his jaw. "Why, he's broke my tooth! Lock him up! He'll get assault for this!"

Was there a twinkle in the eyes of the two tall young men in uniform who marched him away? Briony could not be sure. But in a moment he was again in the cell.

"What is assault?" he asked them.

"You'll find out if you go on as you've begun," one of them said, and suddenly they both burst out laughing. But he heard the grate of the lock in the door. He sat down to wait philosophically as their footsteps died away. What would happen to him? Thank God he was in America, and not Japan! At least the bull-headed man did not have the power of death. When he talked to Mr. Kato he would tell him that over here no one could kill him for dangerous thoughts. That was worth fighting for!

Then suddenly he smelled a perfume. He looked up. It was Allis, waving a scented handkerchief.

"How this place smells!" she said calmly.

"Allis!" he cried. He leaped to his feet.

"Jim," she said, "of all the madness! Why didn't you send for me?"

He went to the door eagerly. She looked like a rose in the morning. "Oh—" he murmured helplessly. "Oh, Allis—I have to explain—"

She stamped her foot on the stone floor. "Jim, why didn't you send for me?"

"Allis, how could I send for you? There is no telephone here, no messenger."

"Everybody in Beechey knows me, silly—you had only to ask for me!"

He pressed his face against the bars. "Allis, never mind about me. Look, those lights were flashing again last night. I saw them myself. I can just see the manse from here."

"I saw them, too," she said. "I telephoned to you and the bell rang over and over again. That's how I knew you weren't at home. Then when the coast guard brought the men in from the sea, and I went to help—of course I heard it."

"What did they do with the men, Allis?" he asked anxiously.

"All saved," she said cheerfully. "We were luckier than usual. The sea was smooth, and it happened so near the shore, that there was time."

"Thank God for that," he said.

A pause fell upon them. He looked at her and saw her red mouth quivering with laughter.

"Jim, how am I going to get you out?"

He grasped the bars in sudden dejection. "Allis, I—I hit the chief in there—you know—"

"Hit him, Jim?" He could see she did not believe him.

"He—he's so thick and red, Allis."

She laughed aloud. "Oh, Jim, if ever I hesitated about you —I never will again! Jim, do you think you can take my money in trust?"

She was laughing but he was not. He was aghast, remembering. "Allis, I'd forgotten, no—look here, all that horrible money—"

"We'll give it away," she said recklessly. "When it's yours

then you have to endow me with it, don't you? Then it'll be mine at last and we'll give it away."

"We could, couldn't we?" he said earnestly. "Yes, that would do. I could give it to you at once and you could give it to anyone you like. But why didn't you think of that before?"

"Why didn't you?" she retorted. She was laughing at him again and loving him. "Maybe I'll only give it to you."

"You dare to look so beautiful," he said severely, "because this damned door is between us and you know I can't get out to kiss you."

"It is going to stay locked," she said, her eyes brimming with her laughter. "It's going to stay locked until I get everything straightened out. But will you marry me the moment you come out?"

He turned a little pale. "Allis, no, don't joke. For a moment, I'd forgotten—I'm not changed—I mean—I am about to start work that I fear you will not approve. Yes, I have quite made up my mind to it. We had perhaps better not decide anything so definite as marriage until—you see, this new work is my duty, and as such it must be done. It is entirely clear to me."

He looked so incredibly good, gazing at her earnestly from behind the prison bars that tears filled her eyes.

"You are such a fool," she murmured, "such a darling fool! Don't tell me anything."

"But Allis—" he protested.

"Keep your cast-iron conscience," she said. "I give up to it. After all these years you're still stronger than I am."

"But, Allis—" he began again.

She leaned forward and put her lips between two bars. "Kiss me," she said.

He waited interminably. He said to himself confidently.

"She will be back in an hour." But an hour was soon gone and then the second hour dragged. At noon food was brought to him and he knew that half the day was gone and she had not come back. No message came. The afternoon wore on to twilight and he was in a fever of uneasiness. But he was helpless. There was nothing that he could do, no way in which he could reach her. At night a man brought soup and bread.

"Could you get a message to someone for me?" he asked diffidently.

"No, I couldn't," the man said gruffly and went away.

Sleep was impossible. When it was dark he climbed on the cot again and clinging to the bars of the small outer window, he gazed once more toward the manse. There were no lights. The church steeple rose black against the starlit sky, and the manse was a lower mass beside it. There was not a light in the house. He clung to the bars until his hands were sore, and then rested and then clung again. Then suddenly, after how long he did not know, he saw the light, very small. He braced himself against the wall, and stared at it. Yes, now it was unmistakable, a clear round beam, such as might come from a small flashlight. It shone out of the attic window, not, he judged, close to the window, but far back in the room, so that the immediate beams would be sheltered by the walls and the ceiling. He watched and counted, three flashes, a space, another flash—tonight the message was different!

"Oh," he groaned. He felt furious with helplessness. There in the house where he lived this was going on!

Then suddenly the whole attic window sprang into light. Someone had come in, someone had turned on the light! Then, as suddenly, the blind was drawn. He could see nothing. Though he kept on watching for another hour, he could see no more. He lay down on his cot exhausted at last and fell asleep.

He was wakened by the grate of his door, dawn had begun to streak his window gray, and he sprang up, confused, brushing his hair back with his hands.

"Jim?" It was Allis's voice.

"Allis," he cried. "Where have you been?"

"You're free, Jim," she said. He had a troubled idea that there was a crowd outside his cell, some police.

"Come out, Jim," Allis said. "They've got someone else to go in your cell."

"You mean—" he said, haltingly. He felt as though he had been years in that narrow room. He came out hesitating.

She put her hand through his arm. "Come, Jim."

"But—but," he said, staring at the men. "Why," he cried, "there's Mrs. Hardman!"

"Good morning, Dr. Briony," Mrs. Hardman said. She looked exactly the same as though she were serving his breakfast.

"What have they got handcuffs on you for?" he demanded. "Why, it's an outrage," he said softly, "first Hasu and then me and now Mrs. Hardman! We can't all be dangerous!"

One of the young men grinned. "We got the right one this time, sir," he said. "Sorry to put you to so much trouble, Reverend," he added.

"Don't you call me reverend," Briony said with sudden irritation.

"The big boss has sure got the swelled jaw this morning," the young man said impudently.

Briony looked shocked. "Has he?" he asked anxiously. "Yes, certainly—I—that was very wrong of me. I don't think I ever struck a man before. The trouble is I learned boxing as a young man. I was very good then—"

"You're very good now," the young man said and laughed.

They were pushing Mrs. Hardman into the door and he saw it.

"But Mrs. Hardman," he cried.

"A tough one," the man said. "Yep, it was her all right. We caught her up in your attic, a flashlight comin' off and on to the sea side. No wonder there's been so many boats blown up passing the cape."

A moment later Mrs. Hardman's gray eyes were blinking at him through the bars.

"Mrs. Hardman," he said. "I can't believe this."

"Can't you, sir?" she said calmly. "I can't hardly myself. But it's true, sir. I've got six ships chalked up that I helped send down."

She put up her hand and with a look of triumph she stared at them as they stood around the locked door.

"Heil Hitler!" she cried clearly.

They were having breakfast together, he and Allis. "You're coming home," she had said firmly, "not to that manse."

So they had come into the quiet house. She had led him upstairs and into a big room that looked to the hills not to the sea. She threw open the closet and there were his few suits hanging.

"I had all your things brought over here," she said.

But now certainly he must tell her that he was committed to that which she might hate very much. She could scarcely like his talking regularly to Mr. Kato not about being enemies but about being friends. That is, he would explain to Mr. Kato that he must tell everyone in Japan that America was not fighting out of hate, but for people to be quite free, even to think their dangerous thoughts.

Then a doubt occurred to him. "Why was I put in jail?" he asked soberly.

"Darling, it was some stupid little man thinking he was being patriotic. He thought he had discovered that Hasu was a spy and that you were aiding and abetting."

"You didn't hear anything about my having dangerous thoughts? It wasn't because of that?"

"No, Jim—have you a dangerous thought?"

He looked at her distressed and yet determined. "I don't know what you would think of it, Allis, but I feel I ought to tell you before—before—"

"Can you give it up if I don't like it, Jim?"

He shook his head so slowly, so ruefully that she laughed and took him by the shoulders and laughed again.

Then she was grave. "This dangerous thought won't take you across an ocean from me again, Jim?"

"No," he said hastily, "no, never—it's not necessary. In fact, I can work better here."

"That's all I want, Jim. That's all I ever wanted—for you to stay with me."

She was gone before he could put out his arms. He was about to follow her when he saw himself by accident in the mirror and was shocked. "How dare I go near her," he thought, "in such a condition of filth!" So he bathed and shaved and dressed himself freshly and then he went downstairs and there she was, waiting for him. "Look," she said and led him to the open doors that gave to the lawn.

"Hasu!" he cried. Yes, there was Hasu, down on his knees searching for weeds. "He won't find as many here as at the manse." He said suddenly, "Allis, how did you get him out?"

"Mrs. Hardman told them he ought to be let out," she said. "When she was caught she confessed everything. She's a German, Jim, and loyal as anything. She isn't really bad—she's devoted and stubborn and she thinks she's right. She gave them such a lecture yesterday—why, she's as stubborn as you are! But she has to be locked up, of course. She's an enemy."

He listened, thinking hard. "Allis," he said, "you don't have to have Hasu here—only if you want him."

"As a matter of fact," she said, "I rather like him. I went to the jail this morning when they let him out—I said I wanted him let out first—so you would feel at home! And of course they let me have my way since I was the one who told them about the lights in the attic. Oh, I'm very popular with the police just now, Jim. Is there anybody you'd like to have locked up? I could do it, you know."

"Are you going to tease me the rest of our lives?" he asked.

But how could she answer? He took her in his arms and held her and kissed her until she was rosy and breathless. Then he remembered something.

"Where's my golden bowl?" he asked.

"I brought that home myself," she said. "There it is on the mantelpiece." Then she looked at him, clarity in her eyes. "This dangerous thought of yours," she said, "has it something to do with the golden bowl?"

"Yes, it has," he said, surprised. "How did you know?"

He went over to the mantel and took down the golden bowl and held it in both hands. They looked at each other over it, dark eyes into blue, and solemnly he recited in Japanese the verse that had been in the bowl when it was given to him.

"Do you want to understand what that says?" he asked.

"No," she said. She took the bowl from him and set it back in its place. There it stood, as it would stand in this house as long as they lived, exquisite against the cream paneling, full of dignity and grace. "This time," she said, "it is enough for me that I understand—you."

She put her soft hand on his lips, as though to seal them. But he put up his own hand and held hers there for his kiss.

India, India

THEY WERE HAVING LUNCHEON at his favorite hotel in London, an occasion he had carefully planned for her birthday. Though he came to London every day, she was not often persuaded to come with him, making the excuse that the city gave her a headache. She could and did work for hours in the garden, coaxing her roses to spectacular bloom, and in so doing forgot all mention of headache, but let him persuade her to meet him in town for luncheon or dinner or for mere shopping and the affliction fell upon them both. For she could never keep her headaches to herself, but must explain to him exactly how her temples throbbed and to such an extent that she could not possibly eat a mouthful.

"We will have luncheon at the Dorchester on your birthday," he had announced a week ago, nevertheless, "and let there be no mention of headaches."

To this she had replied only with her mischievous smile, and that slanting look of her dark eyes which always quickened the beat of his heart. There was no use in hiding from himself the fact that he loved this second wife of his far more than he had loved his first one. Marian had been a good wife to him and an excellent mother to their two sons, now grown, but she had been prosaic. While she had lived he had never thought of the word, and when she died rather suddenly two years ago, he had mourned her deeply. He had taken her for granted for twenty years, and brooding upon their life together, he had wondered if she might have been less prosaic had he not taken her so completely for granted. It was hard for him to remember what she had looked like when he had first married her. Somewhere in the past he seemed to see a rosy cheerful young woman who had made his life comfortable and in doing so had grown into a matron. He had never thought of her dying before him; in her sturdy health he could more easily have thought of her as a widow, mingling with other widows like herself, subdued by their loss, but resolute.

Instead she had died one night in her sleep. He could not believe it, even when she lay so still on the other side of the bed. It was only odd that she had not got up first, as usual. There it was, however, and he and the two boys had been compelled to adjust to her absence. He did not miss her personally so much as he did about the house. She had kept a pleasant house, flowers in vases, fruit in bowls, the cigarette boxes filled, the fires laid and clean towels in the bathrooms. The housekeeper he had got in seemed unable to do any of these things. And when the older boy went back to his job, and the younger to university, it was lonely for him, the deep bottomless loneliness of one accustomed to companionship. And so, when she had been dead a year and he had taken a holiday in Greece, a country he had never visited with her, he had met Laura and fallen in love with her immediately, although she was not in the least like Marian. Perhaps because she was not. She, too, was recovering from death, her husband dead only eight months before of a long illness. When she understood that she was responding again to love she had been horrified.

"Oh, not already," she had cried. "How can I, when—"

He had not allowed her to go on. "Does it matter? Besides, we ought to be glad. It means we can go on living, and together."

She had refused nevertheless to accept him until the full year was ended, and she had even made him go away, lest temptation prove too strong. He had left Greece then, and she had come to England later and they were married quietly in a small old church not far from Westminster Abbey. Neither of them had family, except for his grown sons, and they were plainly relieved that he was to have a home again and said so.

"You're too young to stay a widower," Jonathan, the elder, had said.

But the truth was, and he did not mind now that he had Laura, that the boys wanted to be free to go their own way without responsibility for his loneliness, which, however they might try, they could not alleviate. There was very little that one generation could do for another, and though Laura was nearly fifteen years younger than he, still he could not by any imagination consider that he was old enough to be her father. They were of one generation, even if they were at the extremes, she young enough to enliven his gravity and he old enough to be responsible for her carelessness.

For she was careless, there was no denying it. She left her things about as though she were used to having someone pick them up and put them away, as indeed she was, as she explained when, after some months of marriage, he undertook to reprove her gently.

"Laura, my dear," he said. "Don't you think it would be helpful if you kept some semblance of order in your belongings?"

He was accustomed to an orderly house, for Marian was one of those women who, unobtrusive always, managed nevertheless to hang up coats and hats and to put umbrellas into the stand. He had never to inquire where his galoshes were, for example, because he knew that they would always be on the lower shelf in the closet under the stairs. His housekeeper was not orderly at best, and after Marian died, he had felt a constant irritation at the general state of the house, where dust accumulated and whatever was not put away was left about. He had supposed that when he and Laura came home after their honeymoon that she would of course undertake order as part of her duties as a wife, and he was considerably amazed when she did nothing of the sort. Indeed, she added to the general confusion of the house by leaving her things where she had used them, her garden hat on the chest in the hall, her gloves on the table, the rose clippers outside on the terrace to rust in a summer shower.

At his mild rebuke, spoken in the gentlest way, she had opened her blue eyes very wide. Then she had laughed. "You are quite right," she had agreed frankly. "I am careless. There's no denying it. I got spoiled in India. It was partly Lawrence's fault. He told me not to bother—a servant would always pick things up."

"India is not England," he said.

She agreed again with her usual cheerfulness. "You are right, Leonard."

He had examined her pretty face. Was there a tinge of meaning in her manner? No, he decided there was not. She was humming a song under her breath, a habit that was unconscious with her, apparently. He was not sure whether it meant she was finished with a subject, or ignoring it, or simply feeling nothing. At any rate it always put an end to discussion.

A few days afterward, nevertheless, he undertook to inquire, "Darling," he said, "I love your voice, but must you hum most of the time?"

She had been arranging roses in a bowl in the living room, the one task at which she employed herself regularly. She stopped, her eyes wide again with surprise.

"Am I humming?"

"You were. I don't mind, but it's a bit rude, perhaps. One is not used to it, anyway."

"It is rude," she said quickly. "I quite agree. I'll try to improve."

She did improve, and so quickly that when she began to hum, forgetting, she stopped herself, conscience-stricken, her hand on her mouth.

"Oh, I'm sorry!"

"Never mind," he had said, relenting. "It's rather pleasant. I shouldn't have mentioned it."

"Oh, but you should," she had declared. "Else how would I know? I'm so careless. Lawrence used to scold me, too."

He objected to this coupling with her dead husband. "My dear, I am not scolding you."

"No, but it's the same thing, darling. You're trying to improve me, aren't you? And I don't blame you. I am grateful. I want to be improved. I only wish Lawrence could have done more with me, darling, for your sake."

She had looked at him comically and then had burst out laughing. "Aren't I silly—the idea of his improving me—for you—"

He had been astonished to find himself irritated, and in his irritation he spoke certain unforgivable words. "I wish, Laura, that you wouldn't speak so often of your first husband. It gives me a strange feeling that he is actually here—or at least that you don't forget him."

Her pointed face with its slightly too sharp nose was instantly grave.

"But I cannot forget," she said. "I wouldn't ask you to forget Marian. I don't think you should, indeed. They were a part of our lives, weren't they? In a way they still live in us, don't they? It would be wrong if we do forget them, I think."

This was the beginning of his hideous jealousy. While he

perfectly understood what she meant and indeed agreed with her, he was jealous. She and Lawrence had been the same age. They had grown up in the same town, and had been schoolmates. When Lawrence went to India in the last days of the British Empire, she had followed him within a few months. That meant, did it not, that he and she could not live apart? And if this were so, not only did she remember him, but she cherished his memory, perhaps. He pondered the matter long and secretly, watching her as she moved quickly and gracefully about his house, or if she were languid, as she lay for hours in the June sunshine. She was easily languid in the summer, not from weariness or heat, but from a soft deep yielding of her being that was almost voluptuous.

When winter came she was a different creature. He had been amazed to discover that then she became shivering and irritable. The house was never warm enough, although she wore the warmest clothes and the tip of her nose was always pink. At night, he discovered her feet were cold and had been cold all day. He chafed them in his hands before they went to bed and saw to it that the hot water bottle was re-filled. Yet the winter was not a cold one as English winters go, he had seen much worse, and told her so.

"My dear," he said, "you should exercise more. A good brisk walk would do you good."

"Oh please, Leonard, don't suggest that I go into that dreadful drippy mist."

"The air is fresh," he urged.

"The air is cold," she retorted, "and I hate cold. Even before I went to join Lawrence in India."

The two names in conjunction had decided him. Lawrence and India. He would take her to India and discover for himself where her heart was.

"Darling," he said now as they lunched together at the

Dorchester on her birthday. "Now I shall take you some-where for the rest of the winter—somewhere into the sun-shine. Where shall we go?"

Her face broke into its brightest smile. "To India," she breathed. His heart dropped into silence.

She wanted to go to Ranapur. It seemed that was where she and Lawrence had lived for the five years of their mar-riage, and he did not protest. Let her go where she wished and he would go with her to discover the truth. He took a desolate courage in the fact that Lawrence was dead, while he, Leonard, was alive and married to her. Yet what was the consolation, if her mind and heart were not with him? And Bombay had been beastly hot. They had stayed only two days in the vast old hotel, designed by some empire-minded Englishman, and she could not get away from it fast enough.

"Not Bombay," she insisted. "I don't like Bombay, darling. It's such a mixed-up sort of city, it could be anywhere. Let's go to Ranapur."

One place was the same as another, so far as he was con-cerned, and they went to Ranapur with the incredibly swift transition that jets made possible nowadays. He was surprised to find good accommodations at a new hotel, a converted palace whose bedrooms all had private baths. The palace stood in the middle of a lake and could be reached only by a small boat with a stuttering motor attached to it. What he first considered an inconvenience, however, became within a few days a blessing. The hotel could not be reached by idlers and passersby, nor by the effervescent crowds who wel-comed strangers with enthusiasm and a warmth and kindness which were akin to violence. He discovered their quality al-most at once, for Laura was not at all content to remain within the marble coolness of the hotel palace. She was impa-tient to be out and in the city, restless until he was up in the morning and breakfasted, meanwhile heedless of his astonishment that eggs could be so small and brown, tasting, he declared, of mud, as did the fish served for luncheon and dinner.

"Oh, Leonard, really," she exclaimed, "don't be so English! You can't expect everything to taste the way it does in England because then it wouldn't be India. Lawrence and I ate Indian food on purpose. Food is such a part of the country, he always said."

This was after three days and he retorted firmly. "My dear, I must beg you not to compare me to Lawrence. Allow me to be myself."

She laughed. "Of course, darling. That's what makes you interesting. But I can't help the eggs, can I now? Nor the fact that you won't try a single mouthful of the Indian dishes? Though I assure you they're quite mild, made especially for Englishmen like you. You should at least taste what the Indians themselves eat."

"Why?" he inquired.

She opened those wide eyes. "Perhaps you shouldn't," she agreed.

That she was now a different creature could not be denied. The change was far beyond his imagination. She uncurled herself, body and soul. The shivering pink-nosed woman who had crept about the house in the chill of English winter became in the heat of India a careless and carefree girl. She bloomed in the dry sunshine of the desert city. Her skin was fresh, her lips were red, and her hands and feet were warm as a child's. She consumed oranges until he was alarmed, for he had read somewhere that dysentery germs lurked in the oil folds of the orange skins, heated by the sun.

"Do be careful," he urged. "You shouldn't peel the things and then handle the inside, you know."

"Oh, we did it for years," she insisted, careless of all advice.

She could and did continue to eat with the utmost reckless-ness unspeakable sweets made of soft sugar and cream, of colored pastes and syrups, of pounded nuts and melted butter, and with equal appetite sulfur-colored curries and flavored rice and vegetables which he said also tasted of mud. In spite of all this she was in the highest health, while he, pru-dently remaining as English as possible in his diet, was aware of vague regions of distress inside himself.

"It's because you're fighting," she declared. "You must just give yourself up."

"To what?" he inquired.

"Oh, to things," she made vague answer.

It was not only food. She had innumerable Indian friends, he discovered, persons to whom she chattered in Hindi, shut-ting him out as completely as though he were not present. Now and then she remembered.

"Oh, do forgive me," she exclaimed, her hand on his. "I forget. Lawrence and I really studied, you know. We got quite at ease."

Lawrence and I, Lawrence and I! He found that she had a small photograph of him tucked away somewhere, and was using it as a bookmark. So far as he could see, she had not hidden it. Indeed, it seemed almost accidental that it had been among some old letters, not his, which an Indian friend had found in the house after she left when he died, and had saved until they might meet again. She had explained it to him thus almost indifferently.

"What's this?" he had asked when it dropped from the book she was reading.

"Oh, that—it's a picture of Lawrence when we first came to India. A friend took it."

He studied the handsome young face. It was, he thought, rather arrogant. "Is that how he really looked?"

"Yes, when he was in a good mood. He had a quick temper, though. He could change all in a minute. One never quite knew."

He might never have arrived at the truth had it not been for the Maharanee. For he was well enough known for the Maharana of Ranapur to feel he and Laura should be invited for dinner, although he was not sure whether it was not really because of Laura. Nevertheless with his influence in English business circles, it was quite understandable that the Maharana, a rising young businessman in India, would feel it advisable to cultivate a senior officer in one of the great London banks. His word might go far toward a loan of the sort the Maharana wanted for opening zinc mines in the region.

Throughout the elaborate English dinner, served by three men in white uniforms and scarlet sashes and turbans, he and the Maharana had talked briskly. The Indian, young and modern son of an old prince, had vast plans for his home city of Ranapur.

"We shall skip an age, sir," he proclaimed in his soft, carefully correct English, the consonants blunted, the rhythm so un-English. "We shall move directly and altogether into the jet age. Transport as well, sir, not only passengers, sir. And I shall make Ranapur the great tourist attraction of India, sir. Most modern hotels—how do you find my palace hotel, sir? Comfortable? Very? I hope you will complain to me if anything is less than the best comfort. As for the mines, I shall open not only zinc but some other metals also. These mountains, sir, growing so little of good grass and no forest, nevertheless hide treasures of rare and useful metals. I have geologists here, good scientists, who are telling me, sir, it is the best investment for England to lend us the funds. I should not like to go to Americans before English. And the Russians are pressing us, inviting us with very low interest."

He was quite aware that the dark handsome young man was threatening him gently, and he smiled and replied dryly that as an Englishman and a fellow member of the great Commonwealth, he would appreciate the first opportunity. At this moment, the Maharanee rose, the dinner having concluded with a creamy sweet flavored with almonds, a sickish confection he had tested and left on his plate.

"We will go together into the gold drawing room," she said in her rather colorless, even tones, "since there are only the four of us."

In the gold drawing room she sat down on a long sofa covered in gold brocade while the servants poured coffee into flat gold cups and passed them with plates of sweets. It was his duty, he felt, to devote himself to her for a few minutes at least, since the Maharana had kept him absorbed during dinner. And Laura was exclaiming about the stuffed tigers in the great entrance hall, six of them, and other tigers made into skins and lying on the floors as rugs.

"Tiger country, dear Madam," the Maharana was saying briskly. "I am a hunter and my sons also. We have shooting boxes in the mountains. I shoot every year a few times. Now I shall be too busy, I fear. But we have enough tiger skins, and I shall find other activities more exciting, with your good husband's help."

They drifted out of hearing and he was left with the Maharanee, a slight figure wrapped in a white silk sari. She was no longer young and yet she was not old, pausing in that long period of no change common to women everywhere who are protected from hardship. But she was of a reflective, withdrawn nature as he could see, her dark eyes contemplative and incurious.

"Do you enjoy shooting tigers?" he asked when the Maharana's voice drifted in from the hall. He was describing to Laura the exact method of the sport.

The Maharanee lifted her pale eyelids. "I? Oh no. I am *ahimsa*. I don't believe in killing things."

"Not even tigers?"

She smiled a half smile and put down the small gold cup. "Not even tigers. They don't hurt one unless they are frightened. They creep about in the jungle, quite happy."

"Yet they live by killing."

"Yes, but I am not responsible for what they do—only for myself. I eat no meat."

"Your sons—"

She broke in. "They are no longer children. I am not responsible for them, either—only for myself."

She was not a beautiful woman. It had been, he supposed, one of those arranged marriages. And he could not imagine that the strong, exuberant man to whom she was married could be satisfied with that calm in which she seemed to live. India was full of beautiful women. But she was speaking again.

"I am glad that we are alone for a moment. I want to tell you—your wife is a dear friend of mine."

"Really, your Highness? She hasn't told me."

"Perhaps she does not even know. But she helped me very much once—when I needed help. And so I am glad to see her looking happy and years younger than she looked then. It means you are kind to her."

"I try to be. You see—" he paused. How was it possible to express to this quiet stranger what he felt for Laura? And yet somehow he wanted to do so. "You see, she's very dear to me. I loved my first wife, but Laura is—there's a quality in her of a child who needs happiness or—or perhaps it will die.

There are such children. People are different. Some can grow strong without happiness and—and love. Perhaps they even grow stronger. But others simply—fade and die. I haven't been sure whether I—whether I am the sort of man who can provide the atmosphere in which Laura can well, bloom. I'm much older, for one thing. And I'm a bit fussy perhaps. I try not to be."

The Maharanee made a restless movement of her hands, astonishingly young and swift. Her dark, somewhat sad eyes were suddenly bright. "Don't go on, dear sir," she said with sudden energy. "I assure you that you do provide exactly the right atmosphere for Laura. If you'd only known her first husband. What a cruel, overbearing, impossible—"

The words fell upon his ears like rain upon the desert, benign as blessing.

"Can it be—" he muttered.

"It was so," she insisted.

He listened, his eyes fixed upon her face. Why had he ever thought her plain? She had an inner beauty. Then a thought stayed his ecstasy.

"Why has she never told me?" he inquired.

"I doubt she knows," the Maharanee said calmly. "She was very much in love with him at first, when they were young together. She would laugh at his overbearing ways. She refused to obey him. Then I noticed a change. She did not laugh any more when he criticized her—perhaps because her hair was untidy."

"Ah, she has lovely hair, but soft and thick—difficult, perhaps."

"She began to obey him instead of laughing at him," the Maharanee said. "It was a great change, and I don't think she realized it herself. I noticed it because she began to take refuge in us."

"In you?"

"Not in me, personally. I don't see anyone as much as that. I'm rather a recluse, I'm afraid. I've been reared in loneliness —the only daughter in a palace full of brothers and I was never sent away to school. English governesses are responsible for me. It's made me bad at friendships. No, when I say *us* I mean India."

He was silent, his eyes inquiring and puzzled. She continued, pouring for him another cup of coffee. When he touched her fingers by chance they were cold in their rings of diamonds and emeralds.

"Oh, I know very well what you are thinking. You are remembering our dusty streets and all the little dusty children in their dirty rags of garments. I grant you your thoughts. We may not seem lovable to you. Of course we live in a desert area. Water is scarce everywhere except in the lake that someone made centuries ago by building a dam between two mountains. But the lake belongs to our family, not to the people, although we've always let them wash their clothes and themselves if they liked, on the steps in front of our temple. Still, it's not as though they had water in their houses. And one can't blame them, I suppose, when all the water for the household is carried in a brass pot on a woman's head."

"Of course not," he said, discerning the proud self-defense.

But she was quick to notice the restraint in his reply. "Oh, I know you are thinking that with the money our ancestors poured into these great palaces—well, no one thought of anything else in those days. It gave the people work, I suppose. And my husband, the Maharana—"

"Please," he said. "Were we not talking of my wife? I am so grateful to you for telling me about her."

She recovered her poise. For a moment she was silent. Then again she began to speak quickly, impulsively revealing the very different woman. "Your wife does such beautiful things. She never seems to see the dust on the children, or that they are at all different from—well, from English children. She'll take a child in her arms and hug it to her, rags and dust. I do believe that all she sees is the little thing's face. I remember once she caught a little girl from a gutter and cried out to me, 'Oh, look—did you ever see such eyes? Why do all your children have these glorious eyes?' It is true you know. They all have great dark eyes."

"I have noticed," he said, and forbore to tell her what he had said to Laura only yesterday, when they were walking down a street where there was a bazaar. She had stopped to buy some silver bracelets and the children had crowded about them.

"Laura," he had cried at her, "don't let them touch you!"

"Why not?" she had asked. "They are sweet."

"They are filthy," he had retorted.

"It's clean dust," she had said, "and it must be fun playing in it. I used to play in mud when I was little."

An irrelevant remark, he had thought, and he had shivered when she had put out her hand and rumpled the frowzy head of a small girl until the child was in giggles of joy.

"It wasn't only the children," the Maharanee was saying. "She took refuge in us all, as though she gathered from each of us a flower of love. We love her, you know. Why? Because she doesn't try to improve us. She makes us want to improve ourselves. It's quite different."

He looked at her shrewdly, and felt as though he had known this woman a long time. "Are you trying to teach me something?" he asked frankly.

"Oh no," she said. "I am not so presumptuous nor so naïve. I have nothing to teach you. You will have to find out for yourself why your wife wants to come back to India. Until you do find out, she will want to come back and if you never find out, one day she will come back alone and then she will stay with us forever. You will have lost her."

With this the conversation ended. They sat in silence, she with no more to say, he not knowing what to say, and then the Maharana and Laura were there again.

"The tiger will not hunt man," the Maharana was saying, "unless it has tasted human blood."

"Please," the Maharanee pleaded, "let us not talk of tigers and human blood."

The Maharana laughed. "The Maharanee would have us make pets of the tigers."

It was Laura who took up the defense. "The Maharanee will not commit the sin of inflicting pain."

Between the two women there passed a look of profound understanding.

Wakeful in the night, he pondered what the Maharanee had told him. The bed was a mattress laid on boards, unyielding yet upholding his long thin frame. He was comfortable but without luxury, a situation which invited thought. What was the atmosphere here in this remarkable country which in spite of dust, flies, and a lack of hygiene, provided one, nevertheless, with a feeling of belonging to the human race on a scale that could only be called universal? In London, assuredly, he had his own world, a friendly one, a composite of men like himself, respectable, hardworking, content within a periphery of other persons with whom he had occasional contact. Beyond that he knew there were millions with whom he had nothing in common except the weather which nature compelled them to share. He had no conviction that they were human beings in the same sense that he was one. Here, however, while remaining totally

English, he was becoming aware of being accepted, without his asking or even his wish, into a large human group with whom he would have said he had nothing in common, since he did not like their food nor the way they lived nor could he speak their language. He simply felt they liked him and moreover that they liked him as he was. When he complained that the bath water ran cold, as too often it did, they were eager to make it run hot, and failing, they brought large brass pails of hot water to make amends for the weaknesses of machinery. They divined his wishes before he was able to express them, nor was there ever the slightest criticism of him as being excessive in anything for which he might ask. They made him feel that they enjoyed him as he was. Did he show temper, as twice he had, they looked at him with amazed delight, wagging their heads from left to right, which was their way of agreeing and saying yes, instead of nodding, so that now in retrospect he could not so much as remember what he had showed temper about. Indeed, he felt sufficiently relaxed so that he doubted he would ever show temper again, at least as long as he was in India.

In such mood he fell asleep to wake in the morning in a state of ease which he could not explain until he recalled his conversation with the Maharanee. They were eating breakfast together on their little private terrace of white marble, he and Laura, when he remembered.

"My dear," he said, "I have a confession to make."

"Then why not make it?" she replied.

"Let me preface it by saying how delightful you look in that blue linen frock."

"But, Leonard," she exclaimed, "I never heard you say such a lovely thing before."

"Then I apologize," he said promptly, "for you nearly always look delightful, and when you do not, it is because I have been trying to improve you instead of accepting the truth about you, which is that I married you because you are delightful."

She blushed a fine rose pink. "You confuse me," she said. "I don't know what to make of you, Leonard."

"Darling," he said gently, "why didn't you tell me that Lawrence was cruel to you?"

The rose pink drained away. "How did you know?"

"I am not jealous of him anymore," he replied. "That's how I know. And I know, too, that it isn't because of him that you wanted to come back to India."

"Oh no," she agreed quickly.

"Then why did you want to come back?"

She shook her head.

"You don't know?"

"No," she said, "except here I feel—comforted."

"And you needed to feel comfort because of me."

She bent her head so low that her hair fell over her cheeks. "Perhaps."

"Because I was getting cruel, like Lawrence."

"Not really."

"Oh yes, really."

He reached for her hand across the table and stroked it gently between his. "India has been here a long, long time. It will always be here. And you shall come back as often as you wish—if you feel the need."

A bird came fluttering down from the bougainvillea vine that overhung the terrace. He restrained an involuntary movement to drive it away. When he first did that she had cried out, "Oh, don't send it away—it is used to eating with people."

Now the confident small creature, a swallow of some sort, he thought, a neat little thing in brown feathers and a white breast, clung to the edge of his side plate and pecked at his toast. They sat still until it ate its fill and flew away again. Bird and beast shared human life in this extraordinary land, the monkeys on the walls of housetops of the city and swinging in the trees, the cows ambling along the crowded streets, pausing at the sight of food in a human hand and accepting as a matter of course the proffered bread or fruit or vegetable. He'd seen a cow eat a brown paper bag in which food had been wrapped and this with placid enjoyment. Dogs slept in the middle of the road while man and machine went around them to avoid waking them. Yesterday when he had gone shopping with Laura to buy gifts for his sons, he saw a chipmunk pause on a counter to crack a sunflower seed the shopkeeper offered it.

"Your pet?" he had inquired.

The man had laughed. "I am his pet."

"Now that our bird friend has gone, may I continue?" he asked Laura. "That is, if you are interested?"

"I have never been so interested in my life," she said gravely.

"Then I'll continue," he went on. "I see that my rival in your love is not a man, my darling, but a country. India— India! It is India that you love—I shall have to improve myself, not you. One man, loving you, can I be a match for all this?"

He swept his hands in a gesture that enveloped the marble white city, the palaces, the lakes, the bare beautiful mountains, silver gray against the blue sky. The landscape of romance and of love," he said. "Can I provide it in England?"

He had not been so grave, so uncertain, when he had asked her to marry him as he was now. "Can I hold my own— against India?"

He rested his hands on the table, palms up and open to her hands if she wanted to put them into his.

"You may try," she said and after an instant's hesitation,

she curled her little fists into his hands, waiting palms upward on the table.

Then she looked into his eyes searchingly and straightly, and she moved her head left and right in the Indian affirmation, a gesture he had thought strange until now when he perceived it to be adorable.

"Yes," she said, "yes, you'll hold your own, I do believe, even against India."

Letter from India

"BUT, GOZEAL, it's so absurd to get a letter from someone you can't possibly know," Mrs. Brant said plaintively. "Your father and I think it looks positively queer—especially when it's *India!*"

Gozeal, lying on the high hospital bed, did not reply. Had she not been helpless, the whole correspondence with Nath could have been hidden. She was not at all afraid of her mother—who indeed could fear this gentle and complaining creature? But long ago, even when she was a child, she had learned that life was best when one went one's way alone. It was easier to deal with discovery than with prevention. She did not tell her mother that this was the seventh letter she had received from Nath. The other six were securely under her mattress. The nurse smiled when she tucked them there, but she asked no questions of the quiet woman who was her charge.

As plainly as though she could lift the top of her mother's skull and study the coils of brain stuff there, Gozeal knew what her mother was thinking. A woman of thirty-five, even though her own daughter, a woman who chose to work in a laboratory as a biochemist instead of marrying and having a house and children, such a woman alone would do so strange a thing as welcome a letter from India.

"Nath is a scientist, too, Mother, and scientists don't behave as other people do." Gozeal made her voice careless and she thrust the thick letter under her pillow.

Her mother inquired, "Aren't you going to let me read it to you?"

"Why should we read a letter when you can talk to me?" Gozeal replied.

She wondered in the busy back room of her mind whether this was lying. But what a clutter life would be if the cold truth she loved in the laboratory were the order outside! No, truth was impossible in what was called real life. She put it away.

"Tell me about the new greenhouse," she said mildly. Her mother's passion for flowers provided ample material for the length of the visit allowed her—half an hour.

"The heating isn't what it should be," her mother began with the faint hurry that signified her interest. "I wish now I had not been tempted by electricity. But the plumber saying the furnace was already overloaded—"

Gozeal, lying motionless upon the bed, felt life intolerable. Withdrawing her attention from her mother, while she continued to look at her, she went over again, as she had done so many times before, what it was that she had done so stupidly on that bright spring day, now six months and seven days ago. She had felt unusually well and happy. The early morning walk to the laboratory had been delightful, and for one moment she had lingered upon the threshold of the building, surprised to find that she wished she need not go in. To her own embarrassment she thought of another day, long before, when on such a spring morning she had run away from work to spend the whole day on the river with Bruce. She had shrugged her shoulders at the memory and had gone in and begun work quickly. It was at the end of that earlier day when she knew she must not marry Bruce or any other man. In the midst of that earlier spring, when she had been only twenty-five, she had been amused to find that not even Bruce could keep her from dreaming of the long experiment, to which, if she committed herself, she must devote the rest of her life. She had let him kiss her and she had kissed him, and then she had told him bluntly, "You deserve a real wife—not me. I shan't marry you, Bruce."

Through all his argument and final passion she had been resolute. Once the determination was made, it was easy to keep it, because she was doing what she wanted to do.

"But my real problem is old Martin," her mother was saying. "He will keep making more and more begonias and those things with spotted leaves. What is the use of a greenhouse full of pale begonias and spotted leaves?"

"None," Gozeal said. "Why don't you throw them out?"

"I can't bear to hurt his feelings," her mother replied.

She had hurt Bruce ruthlessly and she had never been sorry. Ten years had passed as a dream. But she had withdrawn more and more into the laboratory, shielding herself from questioning eyes. Not to marry at all was to make herself peculiar. After Bruce had gone, and especially after he had married little Roberta Williams, whom everybody called Bobbie, it had not seemed worthwhile even to accept such invitations as came her way. The experiment was absorbing her, body and soul. Into the tiny hormones of universal life she had delved, discovering, or almost discovering, the secret of their creative union. She had passed Bobbie on the street one day, obviously about to have a baby, and she had nodded and smiled without speaking. The irony of life was that women like Bobbie, little creatures less than nothing, could create within themselves the life which she pursued so relentlessly under her microscope. Impatient with the best of those instruments, she had taken a year from the experiment to invent, patent, and manufacture a superlative instrument of her own—the Brant Double Lens Super-microscope, it was called. Well, it was paying her endless hospital bills.

But how had it happened that the secret she had so nearly

discovered had turned on her that bright spring day and had so nearly destroyed her? Step by step she went over the familiar process. She had combined her F element and her M element, exactly as she had before, but in a new and surely harmless solution, and then there had been the explosion. When it was over for her, she found herself lying in this bed, bandaged from head to foot, facing blindness. She would not be totally blind. If she focused her eyes carefully now, she could almost distinguish her mother's small pretty features. That was no test, of course. She knew so well how her mother looked.

"Well," her mother said, "my half hour is up."

The nurse came in and Mrs. Brant rose and went over to the bed and put her hand upon her daughter's scarred one. Upon her hand Gozeal felt that convulsive pressure which meant that her mother was near to tears. She smiled at her mother, seeing her dimly pale.

"Don't worry about me," she said clearly. She wanted no worry. It would be easy to put an end to her life as soon as she could be alone again. Science was proficient in death, if not in creating life.

When her mother was gone she reached under her pillow and brought out the letter. "Have we time for this before the trays?" she asked the nurse. The worst of life was to have it scheduled by trays of food she did not want to eat.

But the nurse was kind. Moreover, she had a curiosity about the letters from India and their effect upon the tall silent woman who lay so patiently through hours of pain. "You'll eat better, I guess, if I read you that letter," she said.

Gozeal handed her the letter without speaking. When she could see for herself Nath's handwriting again, she would be well enough to die. Now she closed her eyes and fixed her mind. All her trained attention concentrated on what she was about to hear. The nurse was opening the letter, rustling the pages, clearing her throat—Gozeal had learned to forget the light vulgar little voice, utttering the profound words. The letter began without salutation, as all his letters did:

"I sit this morning in the small pavilion which I have built near my house. As I told you, I can be alone here, not because I have forbidden anyone, but because the walk across the hot earth is enough to prevent the idle. You will receive this letter without much delay, for your last letter has made me anxious. The writing was entirely legible—do not apologize. I had rather have your own handwriting, even as it is, than that of another. But I felt you weakening in your courage. Therefore I have put aside my own work today. My laboratory door I have locked. I come to the aid of your spirit."

"Stop a moment," Gozeal said.

In the silence while the nurse paused Gozeal repeated to herself these words. "He comes to the aid of my spirit!"

"Do you feel worse?" the nurse inquired.

"No," Gozeal replied. "Please go on."

"I ask you to remember our meeting," Nath wrote. "It was not by chance. I sent a letter to an unknown address, in reply to an article that an unknown white man had written in a magazine which fell into my hands. But that man was not important. He was merely the conveyor. Through him a letter fell into your hands. It was my letter. Had that other one answered it, there would have been an end. But you answered. This was by divine design. I, who felt the whole western world hateful and corrupt, who wrote in anger and scorn because a white man had once more maligned my people, I who expected from him an angry reply, received instead your benign and thoughtful letter. For the first time I understood that in your western world there could be one like you."

"Please," Gozeal said, "I will rest a moment."

"Maybe we had better finish after your tray," the nurse suggested.

Gozeal shook her head slightly and did not speak. The argument with Ray Barclay had been a stupid one. Pure scientist that she was, she had resented his slashing judgments on India without herself knowing anything about the country. A doctor, who had spent his one year there in an American camp, listening to white men and looking at the beggars swarming to grasp at any refuse thrown away, Ray had come back to condemn the whole of India as a nation of people scarcely worth keeping alive.

"I read somewhere that there was a famine in Bengal that year you were there," she had said.

They were working on a test injection that morning. The volunteer, a broadbacked young medical student, groaned. "We had better do our job instead of arguing about a country so far away it doesn't matter to us anyway," Ray had replied.

When letters began to come from India protesting the article he later wrote and published, he had thrown them away. Thus he had tossed aside Nath's letter one day in the office, and she had seized upon it. "What is this stamp?" she had asked.

"India," he had replied carelessly, "a kickback—I'm getting them."

"Aren't you going to answer it?" she had asked.

"Why should I?" he had retorted.

Something in her scientist's soul had stirred against this, too. Impartiality was justice, and justice should not be used only for the relations of germs and hormones. It was a principle or it was nothing. Science ought, to be worthy of itself, to reach to the very limits of the universe, human as well as material.

"Do you mind if I read it?" she had asked.

"Take it," he said indifferently. "I was only going to throw it away. You might give me the stamp, for my boy's collection."

She had torn off the stamp, and then during her lunch hour, which meant a sandwich eaten at her laboratory table, she had read Nath's letter. Three letters of Nath's she had read with her own eyes.

"All right," she said aloud to the nurse.

"That you are woman instead of man makes no difference to me," Nath wrote. "Whether we meet in the flesh matters nothing. You healed my soul. What I have not told you, I will now tell you. Why do I say you? I have not told anyone what I now tell you.

"You know that I am not a person of great consequence. That is, I am neither Gandhi nor Nehru, but in my own way as a scientist, I am a person, too, at least here in my own province. My father was one of those who in the last generation believed in tolerance toward the white man. We were taught, my brother and I, that even as many peoples had come into India through the thousands of years of our history, and all had stayed in peace and friendliness, so now was the English white man come. You know that long before these, there had come other white men, entering at our north. They were the early white tribes of Europe, wandering eastward. Although at that time we were already a civilized people, understanding more than a little of science, even those we received and they became part of us.

"But when I went to the provincial college to study western science, I learned to hate a white man there, the only one I knew until then. Arrogant, narrow, and proud, he nevertheless was in authority over me. He knew my hatred and he managed unjustly to send me away, and I came back to my father's village in shame and despair. I determined to bury myself among my own people, to work alone. You know I married the woman chosen for me and that by her I have had four children, of whom two are living. My elder son is now twelve years old.

"Who can divine destiny? That white man, rising in favor with the authorities, was sent here as our governor. I had to meet him time after time, as the one elected by my people to present their cases to him when he was angry for some fault or other. At every turn he despised me and refused me. I lost the confidence of my people. When I read the words of Barclay, I determined to kill this white man here, even though it cost my life.

"You must understand that such a determination on my part was a great sin. Our religion does not allow us to kill even the lowest creature. Yet I was ready to lose my own soul, in my great hatred. But before I was ready to kill this white man, I wished also to express my indignation to the unknown white man, for his injustice toward my people. I expected no reply and I went about the plan for my destruction. It was not difficult. I would do it alone, for I wished to endanger no other creature. Afterward I would give myself up, proudly acknowledging that it was I who had committed the crime. I understood the making of hand grenades. I would make a grenade and when next I went to plead the case of one of my people, I would throw the grenade at my enemy, who was the judge. I am strong and my hand is accurate. No one would suspect me or search me. I justified myself by believing that the grenade was to be thrown not only for myself, but for all my people, who have been so long despised by western men.

"Then came your letter. I shall never forget the day. The letter was put into my hands by my elder son. He was curi-

Letter from India • 149

ous about it, he wanted to know what country it came from. We discovered this from the stamp. Then I opened the letter, expecting it to be the angry reply to my letter. Instead your quiet words met my eyes. 'Dear unknown friend.' I can repeat the whole letter by heart. I sent my son away, and I read it over and over again alone. And as I read there came over my soul the full knowledge of how great was the injustice of the crime I planned to commit. The mercy and the understanding contained in your words overwhelmed me, and I trembled and wept. Had I fulfilled my plan, it would have been a crime against you. While you lived, I could not hate. It would have been too great an injustice.

"Now, after this year in which we have come to know one another's minds, I can only thank you that out of the justice of your own soul you saved me, and not only me, dear friend whom I now know, but my family and my village, and far beyond that. Because of you, I have been able, within my small influence, to help my people to remember that this evil white man is only one creature, and that there is one like you. You tell me that there are many like you. Can it be so! But if there is only one, hatred is impossible. When some here have cried out their hatred, I have taken the great liberty to read to them your letters, especially the first one and then the third one, wherein we discussed the nature of the human heart. Under the sublime justice of your words, our hatred has died away and we have been strengthened to endure.

"When your own sorrow fell upon you, how grateful was I that now I could comfort you! Count upon me, dear one. I am Nath, your friend. We are all your friends, here in our village. My wife loves you and my children take pride in you. I hesitate to say this, that I am about to say, for our village is a simple one and our home is not rich—certainly very poor in comparison to the pictures I have seen of your country. But should it be that you cannot return to your work, then come to us. What we eat shall be yours and all that we have is yours, as long as you live.

"This is much more than gratitude, although I of all men am grateful to you. You saved my soul. Let me restore yours, by any way I can, for what I owe you. For one thing I know —design, not chance, rules our lives."

The nurse paused.

"Is that all?" Gozeal asked.

"That's all," the nurse said. She laughed. "Gosh, I guess that's one invitation you won't want to accept. Snakes and spiders everywhere, I'll bet! You ready for your tray?"

"Yes, thank you," Gozeal said.

The nurse gave her the letter and went away and Gozeal lay with the letter warm in her hand. She could see Nath as clearly as if he stood here in the room, Nath and his little family, he tall and spare, his wife at his side, and the two boys. Design, not chance, rules our lives. Scientist that she was, she knew it to be true. She had been trying to discover the design of life when the accident came. But the design was still there, design far deeper than that of two chemical elements, exploding when they touched. Suddenly she wanted to live. She would write to Nath and tell him she wanted to live.

The nurse bustled in with the tray. "Hungry?" she asked in her formula.

"Yes!" Gozeal exclaimed in true surprise. "I believe I am—at last!"

To Whom a Child Is Born

AMERICA—1960s

"ELIZABETH!"

She was at her desk but she recognized the urgency in Michelle's voice. She had learned to weigh the exact measure of this urgency, for Michelle's French mother had endowed her with a warm, urgent voice. One had to weigh whether it was the urgency of joy, pleading, anxiety, a number of different possibilities. This morning it was a mixture of pleading and passion. Therefore she made her own tones calm and cautious.

"Yes, Michelle?"

"Are you very, very busy?"

"As usual."

Michelle paused, her large dark eyes dramatic. "Then may I—"

"Is it man, woman, or child?" she inquired.

Thus encouraged, Michelle advanced into the room.

"A girl, Elizabeth—a beautiful Japanese girl!"

"How far along?"

"Three months."

"You are the caseworker, Michelle. Can you not handle the matter yourself?"

"Elizabeth, certainly I can! Do I not so every day? But this is one unusual. The father is also Japanese, Elizabeth— two families Japanese but Americans also, and intellectual, well respected. The young man was a war hero, in Italy. Everything is good. But—"

Michelle flung out her hands, lifted her fine eyebrows, and gave the famous shrug.

"But what?" Elizabeth inquired, still calm, still cautious. She had been out late last night on a case involving a woman who had deserted her family of three small children in a railroad station. It was long after midnight before the children were in a house of shelter, and she could go home to her own apartment and to bed. This morning she was tired and somewhat dispirited by humanity. The procession of displaced, misplaced children, all helpless, seemed endless.

"He does not wish to proceed with the marriage, this hero!" Michelle's voice of outrage implied indignation with scorn of the male sex, an attitude contradicted by her warm beauty.

"Does he know he is the father of this child?"

"Oh yes, he knows indeed, and it is the reason."

"The reason for what?"

"Why he says he cannot marry the girl."

Elizabeth put down her pen. She knew very well the complexities of following Michelle's delightfully illogical mind.

"I had better shorten this discussion and see the girl for myself."

"It is what I hoped," Michelle replied gratefully.

She left the room to reappear almost at once with a slender Japanese girl in a dark green tailored suit, a shy, graceful girl, not pretty until one really looked at her. Then one perceived the perfection of the oval face, the clear pale skin, the long eyes, the delicate mouth. She carried herself with a melancholy grace.

"Miss Anderson, this is Mariko Tanaka," Michelle said.

Elizabeth put out her hand. "Please sit down."

The girl's hand was small and soft and cold. She sat down,

clasped her hands together tightly in her lap, and remained silent and motionless, her eyes downcast.

"How can we help you?" Elizabeth inquired gently.

Many young girls had sat there in the brown armchair and each had been different. Most of them, however, were eager to tell their story. This girl was not.

"You would like us to place your baby for adoption?" she asked in the same gentle voice.

The girl lifted her eyes. "Yes." She considered a moment and went on. "I hope there are good parents for a Japanese baby."

One would not have known that she was Japanese from the way she spoke. Her accent was American, Boston bred and pure. She had been given a good education. No ring on that third finger of the left hand, however!

"There are always good parents for any baby. It is our duty to find them. Don't worry about that."

The girl looked down again and continued silent.

"Do you have a family?" Elizabeth asked at last.

"I am not their responsibility," the girl said.

"I think your family should know, don't you?" Elizabeth put the question gently but firmly.

The girl was reluctant. "My mother knows."

"And approves of your giving up your baby?"

"It is necessary."

In the silence again, Elizabeth felt the powerful pull of Michelle's gaze. The two women exchanged looks and she turned to the girl.

"I had better have a talk with your mother."

"She will not come here," the girl murmured.

"Then I will go to her. It is absolutely necessary that I see her before we proceed with this adoption. One doesn't just discard a child."

The girl lifted her head. "Oh no, please," she gasped. "I will—I will bring her here—somehow."

"When?"

"Tomorrow."

Outside the agency door, Mariko Tanaka hesitated. She had asked Tomio to meet her at the small park where they had met so often, at eleven o'clock, she had said, and now it was a quarter past the hour. He was impatient by nature, and he might not have waited, especially as he had been reluctant to see her again, when she telephoned him early this morning.

"What is the use?" he had said. "We have decided to call it all off."

"I may have something to tell you."

"You aren't thinking of—"

"No, it's too late for that. The doctor said so. Please, Tomio! Besides, how shall we tell my father? We haven't talked about that."

"I shall simply tell him I've changed my mind."

"Oh, that won't save him from the most awful disappointment! I wish I were dead."

"It might make things more simple," he agreed grimly.

Used as she was to his moods, she had been stunned by this and then angered. "Well, let me tell you I shan't kill myself, nevertheless! Will you be at the park, Tomio?"

"Yes."

She saw him now on the park bench under the sycamore tree as he had been so many other times, exactly as though nothing had happened between them. He rose when she came near and stood rather formally until she sat down. They did not touch hands, and she looked at him appraisingly, as though she had not seen him for years instead of days, and he, catching her look, pretended he had not.

"Look at those two sparrows," he said, "fighting over a dead beetle! I've been watching them for the last ten minutes."

She laughed. "Silly little things!"

They were diverted for a moment, watching the minuscules.

"Well," he said at last, his eyes still fixed on the sparrows, "what's the big news?"

"You needn't worry any more about the—the—baby."

He turned his head to her sharply. "What do you mean not worry? You haven't decided on an—an operation?"

"I told you, it's too late for that."

"Well?"

"I simply mean I've arranged everything."

"But what?"

"Does it matter? You didn't ask before what I was to do. You just said you couldn't go on with—with me."

"And now I can, you mean."

"If you wish—"

"Or if you wish—"

She did not answer this. She stooped and threw a pebble at the quarreling sparrows. They flew away in opposite directions, leaving the beetle behind.

He went on. "We're different people, somehow. You're not the person I thought you were—I'm not what I thought I was."

"Perhaps it's better as it is," she agreed and then added half sadly, "I wish my father needn't be hurt."

"I've thought of that," he said. "I could just say I must go to Japan first, to take my parents' ashes home to the ancestral burial plot. Then, while I was gone, you might find someone else—"

"Or you might."

"Not me."

The change in his voice made her glance at his profile. His handsome mouth was set and she saw the pulse beating in his cheek. If only she could understand him! Yet she did understand him in a curious blood-deep sort of way . . . Then— if only she had never yielded to him, if only she had remembered the teachings of her mother and her grandmother and the generations of women before! But they were Japanese and she was American and American women were free. Were they not? Then why the punishment? Oh, poor little baby unborn!

At the thought of the child her veins filled with bitterness. She tasted bitterness even in her mouth, as though a bitter bile flowed through her, a female bitterness directed against him. She rose and flicked the sharp nails of her thumb and forefinger against his cheek.

"Goodbye," she said. "If ever you know what you want to do, then let me know. I might want to do the same thing—or I might not. Anyway, then we'd both know."

She walked away from him as swiftly as she had come and tried not to look back. But at the last turn of the path she did look back. He was sitting there, looking after her, and she turned away again and walked on and out of sight.

"There's no Mrs. Tanaka, it seems," Elizabeth said, when the next day was nearing noon.

In the coming and going of people wanting to adopt children and other people wanting to give children away, the office had been its usual center of human interchange, tragic and happy. She had maintained her central judicious calm, flanked by Michelle's mercurial despair and hopefulness. Both women had looked often out of the window for Mariko and her mother but they did not appear. The office was enlivened now by flashes of unexpected spring lightning and grumblings of thunder on the horizon. Rain fell with sudden fury and stopped when the clouds shifted to reveal blue depths beyond, an April day, the atmospheric pressure unstable.

Elizabeth continued, "Perhaps they have found their own solution."

"It is not possible, that," Michelle retorted. "I am much more afraid Mariko will kill herself because her mother will not come and nothing can be done. Japanese have some strange inside stubbornness, I think."

"You always think the worst will happen, if the best immediately does not," Elizabeth reminded her.

"And am I always wrong?" Michelle demanded.

"You are nearly always right," Elizabeth replied, "and I am going out for a while."

"Where?" Michelle inquired.

"I have an errand," she replied.

"Do you wish to buy a hat?" Michelle inquired with malice, her brown eyes bright. "I hope so, Elizabeth, for indeed that thing you continue to wear on your head is disgrace, even to a social worker."

"Thank you for telling me," she replied, smiling, and put on her jacket and the despised hat. The errand was private and against her principles.

She was going to the Tanaka house, to see for herself what was to be seen, though slightly uncomfortable as she always was when she undertook these personal investigations to families. Deeper than discomfort, however, was her almost religious belief that a child should remain with its natural parents, if at all possible. If it were impossible, then she could enjoy finding the substitute family, the adoptive parents—playing God, as Michelle teasingly put it.

She took a cab now and rode for ten minutes or so. Then she paid the cabby and got out. The street was old, and the house was old, one of the small pleasant houses of old Boston, still beautiful, though squeezed between two tall new buildings. She mounted the steps, very scrubbed and clean as she noticed, and rang the doorbell. It was answered by Mariko herself.

"May I come in?" she said gently.

"Oh—Miss Anderson!"

The lovely Japanese face paled with consternation. "Please —my father is at home."

"I came to see your mother," she said, and waited, immovable.

"Please, wait a minute—"

The girl disappeared and she stepped inside the narrow hall. To the left a long living room stretched the depth of the house. It was pleasantly furnished with a mixture of Japanese and American effects. Above the carved white chimneypiece was a scroll painting of willows in spring, under which a crane stood on one leg. To the right was a library, or a study, the desk piled with books. A handful of writing brushes were collected in a bowl beside a typewriter.

The door at the end of the hall opened and a slender middle-aged woman came in. She had on a neat black suit and a small ruffled white apron which she untied as she came in, and her black hair, thinning at the temples, was pulled back from her delicate, anxious face.

"Miss Anderson, I am Mrs. Tanaka." She had an unusually soft voice. "Please, come into the living room."

She led the way into the room, and toward the back, so that they could be unseen from the front door.

"I am sorry to interrupt your luncheon," Elizabeth said as she sat down.

"Oh no," Mrs. Tanaka said in the same soft hurried voice. "I eat only a little at noon. Usually my husband eats at the university, but today he forgot some papers and came back, and so I prepared something. Mariko will attend to him now. He is going soon. He has a class."

She stopped, her eyes on Elizabeth's face. As clearly as though she had asked, the question hovered in the air between them: "Why are you here?"

"Mrs. Tanaka," Elizabeth said, "your daughter came to our offices yesterday."

Mrs. Tanaka's lips quivered. She turned her head to listen for some other voice, or footstep, beyond this room. Elizabeth paused involuntarily. A man was speaking somewhere, calling from another room, or possibly from the stairs.

"Hai, Mariko! Where is your mother?"

The voice was imperious but kind.

"Excuse me," Mrs. Tanaka exclaimed and hurried from the room.

Elizabeth waited. The two women's voices spoke Japanese and English together. The man's voice ended the conversation.

"Enough, enough!"

He was evidently going upstairs. She heard firm footsteps. Then Mrs. Tanaka hurried into the room again, her cheeks faintly flushed. "He lost his fountain pen," she explained. "He loses small things easily and then—we all must look."

She smiled in apology, and sat down, breathing too quickly.

"It is quite all right," Elizabeth replied. "As I was saying, your daughter came to us with a strange story. Mrs. Tanaka, I cannot believe that she and her fiancée—"

"He is no longer her fiancée," Mrs. Tanaka said. "Everything is now impossible."

"That is what I cannot believe," Elizabeth said firmly.

She had said so many things firmly in the course of the years that she had acquired a tranquil stubbornness. But Mrs. Tanaka was equally stubborn, though always gentle.

"It is difficult for you, an American lady, to understand altogether," she said with courtesy. "Yet there are some matters which can never be explained to you, because there is not the same experience behind explanation. We are Japanese."

"You live here," Elizabeth reminded her. "You should behave here as Americans."

"We are only Japanese American," Mrs. Tanaka maintained.

The footsteps were coming downstairs.

"Excuse me," Mrs. Tanaka said. She hastened away, half running.

Elizabeth waited again. What sort of a monster was he, this Dr. Tanaka, of whom they were all afraid, it seemed? She considered walking across the room and meeting him boldly and thus forcing a real conference between parents and daughter and herself. Why not? She rose, but before she could take a step Mariko came in, agitated, glancing behind her.

"Please, my mother will come at once. My father is asking her to come with him to buy something—a new shirt—he wants for some occasion tonight—"

"I would like to meet your father," she said.

"Oh no—" Mariko's face went pale.

Elizabeth insisted. "Wouldn't it be the natural, easy way to—"

"I would kill myself—"

There was no mistaking the girl's desperate anxiety. She could only sit down again. Outside in the hall a conversation was going on in English.

"Who is your visitor?"

"A woman—a stranger—" Mrs. Tanaka was fumbling.

"Then why is she here?"

"Perhaps selling something—I don't know—you will be late—"

"I have three quarters of an hour. I shall work for a short time here at my desk, review some notes that—"

The voice was not unkind, not even very curious, a professor's voice. It went on.

"Has Tomio called today?"

"No, I think not. Perhaps Mariko—"

"When he calls tell him I would like him to come to the dinner tomorrow night. It will be a learned occasion. I want to present him—to my colleagues."

The voice faded and a door shut.

"He has gone into his study," Mariko said under her breath.

"Please excuse me." Mrs. Tanaka came into the room.

Mariko rose but Elizabeth stopped her.

"Please stay, Mariko. Let's talk this over together."

Mother and daughter exchanged looks.

"Why are you so afraid of him?" Elizabeth asked.

"We are not afraid of him, Miss Anderson," Mariko said. She was seated now in a pale green velvet chair, her eyes on the door. "We are not afraid of him," she repeated. "We only—love him."

Elizabeth looked at the two exquisite and stubborn women and tried again.

"Are you the only child, Mariko?"

Mrs. Tanaka answered for her. "Oh no—I have five daughters. Mariko is the eldest. I have no son."

"It is our problem," Mariko said.

"Can a good family be a problem?"

Elizabeth put the question half playfully, but with serious

intent. The girl hesitated, glanced at her and back to the door again. "It is a problem in a Japanese family—an old-fashioned family—if there is no son. My father—well, actually he is quite a famous man, both here and in Japan. He is a philologist—internationally known. When I—when my fiancée—when Tomio and I fell in love, my father was very happy. He wished Tomio to become his son legally. It is an old Japanese custom when there is no son, the husband of the eldest daughter may take the family name. It was so arranged—"

A smile, edged with sadness, now flickered over Mrs. Tanaka's face.

"We had an announcement party here in our house—all our friends were here and my father in the middle of the party, when all the guests were laughing and talking, he got up and told everybody that he had invited Tomio Nagai to be his legal son, and that Tomio had accepted."

Tomio Nagai! She remembered the name, the young man had indeed won high honors in the battle at Anzio, Italy.

"Does Tomio Nagai have a family?"

"He has not," Mrs. Tanaka replied. "His parents died in the desert camp in Arizona. They were old. Tomio is the youngest and he stayed here when the war began. His brothers and sisters chose to return to Japan. But his father was an artist. He could not adjust. He had lived his whole life in America."

Mariko interrupted, forgetting the door. "Mother, why do you say they died? His father killed himself, Miss Anderson, and the mother took poison. Tomio was in Italy fighting for the Americans and he did not know how they died—not until he came back again, and was given the medal for extraordinary bravery on the battlefield. He respects my father very much. That is why—perhaps—" Her voice trailed into silence.

A door opened briskly into the hall.

"Father!" Mariko whispered. Mrs. Tanaka rose at once and both mother and daughter went into the hall.

She was alone again in the strangeness of this house. What was the power Dr. Tanaka had over his family? Why were they determined to hide the truth from him? If he knew, if he were helped to understand, he might approve, after all, even accept the child—

Yet affectionate family talk now floated into the room. He was speaking.

"Mariko, drink a little more milk. You are looking too pale these days. Love is too much for you, I think!"

He was laughing and teasing.

"You must not let yourself grow thinner, you know! We Japanese men don't like our women too thin . . . Hana, my black silk socks—a hole—"

"I know, I will mend them. Everything will be ready for tomorrow night. Shall I type your speech again?"

"No, no—I can read the notes on the margin—you do too much, as it is."

The front door opened and closed. She heard nothing for a moment, and knew that the two women were preparing themselves to face her again. Indeed she must discover the truth.

They came in and sat down now very near her. Mrs. Tanaka spoke and obviously by agreement in that brief moment in the hall it had been decided between them that the mother was to speak first. "I will try to explain to you, Miss Anderson, why we cannot—why the child is not—acceptable. In our family, that is—"

"I should like very much to know," Elizabeth replied. She bit back other words which crowded to be spoken. The child, she would like to have said, the innocent child is nevertheless a member of your family. She had learned long ago not to speak too soon.

"The reason goes back many years," Mrs. Tanaka said after a pause. "You are American. It may not be possible for you to understand even if I tell you. I don't know where to begin . . . Let me begin with myself."

She moistened her pale lips and went on. "Miss Anderson, please understand. For Japanese women, especially of my generation, the hope of success in marriage is to give the husband a son."

She paused so long now that Elizabeth felt it necessary to encourage her.

"It's natural to want both sons and daughters."

"It is more than that," Mrs. Tanaka replied. "It is essential for a man to have a son. Otherwise how can the family be carried on to new generations? Our family is very old. We are not common. My husband's young brother was killed in the Pacific during the war. He was an officer in the Japanese navy. Yes, he returned to Japan rather than submit to the desert camps. We went to the camps. We knew the parents of Tomio Nagai there. A distinguished artist, his father was. We were able to—to—see that the funeral was—suitable. His wife—died alone. They were buried together."

She paused. Her pale face went a shade paler, but she did not falter. "I tell you this not to complain of bitterness, but to explain why my husband was so happy to announce that Tomio would be his legal son. This was even more important to him than marriage to Mariko. You would have to be Japanese to understand this."

"I can understand, at least partly," Elizabeth said. "There are many men who want a son when they don't have one. But does the fact that a child has been conceived—too early, let us say—mean that Tomio Nagai cannot be a son to your family?"

"Now I must explain Tomio also," Mrs. Tanaka said. "He

is very proud—doubly proud, for he is a hero as an American, but as a Japanese he is also proud. He cannot disgrace our family with a child of the sort we call 'wild.' What you call illegitimate we call 'wild,' that is, outside the family. This child can never be inside the family. Tomio feels he has disgraced my husband. He is not worthy to be our son. For this he blames Mariko. He does not wish to marry her."

"Blames Mariko!" Elizabeth exclaimed.

"It is really Mariko's fault," Mrs. Tanaka said. "It is always the woman's fault. She should be strong."

There was a pause while the two women looked at each other. Neither yielded. Mariko was crying silently, her face turned away.

"But you—" Elizabeth said, and stopped.

For the first time a faint color changed the pallor of Mrs. Tanaka's face. "Miss Anderson," she said almost impulsively. "I cannot hurt my husband. If it were not for his generosity, I would not be here now. He saved my life. I will tell you—"

The story was a long one, and Mrs. Tanaka told it with grateful tenderness. There was no doubt that she loved her husband, had loved him from the very day she saw him, and this in spite of the fact that theirs had been an arranged marriage. What chagrin then, when one after the other she had presented him with three daughters!

"One after the other," she said, wincing, "and one each year because I thought surely there would be a son, but there was not. In six years we had five daughters. He was very kind, Miss Anderson. He loved his daughters. But I could see that he was disappointed very much so. Yet he did not reproach me."

"I hope he knew it was not your fault," Elizabeth said dryly.

"Oh, he never reproached me," Mrs. Tanaka repeated,

"but it was I—I—who reproached myself. Other women have sons, why not I? I am bad luck for him, that's what I said to myself. So I tried again. It was too soon. I was tired from many children. I knew I was not well enough. When I went to the hospital I was frightened for myself. I did not tell him. No use to worry the husband then, when the child has to be born. It was very difficult."

She told the story well and, curiously, not from her own point of view but from his. He was, she said, good, as an American husband is good. He went to the hospital with her and waited while the birth took place. There was no one else in the waiting room then, for it was three o'clock in the morning. He had tried to read a magazine, but he could not. He was expecting to be told that he had a son at last, yet was afraid that he had a sixth daughter. Suddenly, when it seemed he could not wait any longer, the doctor had come in, very grave.

"Dr. Tanaka," he said, "I have a serious situation. Your wife is not responding well. We are approaching a crisis. I must have a swift decision from you. I cannot save both the mother and the child. Which shall I save?"

He had never thought of such a possibility. To decide whether his wife should die—or his son—if it were a son! He was ashamed to put the question to an American. But there was no time to explain the importance of a son to his family. His parents were dead. He was an only son. If he never had a son—

"Is the child a—son?"

"It is too soon to tell," the doctor had replied. "And no time to wait," he had added.

Mrs. Tanaka looked appealingly at Elizabeth.

"Think of my poor husband," she pleaded. "Think of his suffering! To condemn his wife to death—perhaps when the child is not a son! If the child were a son, could he give permission for his death?"

Dr. Tanaka, it appeared, had asked indeed one more question. While the doctor waited, watch in hand, he had asked it.

"If I could be sure that my wife is bearing a son—"

"We cannot be sure," the doctor had replied. "The child is not born yet."

"But there may be another chance, at that, may there not?"

"There will not be another chance," the doctor had replied. "Your wife must never have another pregnancy. It would cost her life."

Dr. Tanaka had broken at that. His face had wrinkled with suppressed weeping. He thought of his good wife, of her unselfishness, her devotion. No, he could not live without her. Besides, what would he do alone with all those daughters?

"Save her life," he had whispered.

"Good," the doctor had said, and had sped away.

As it turned out, the child had not been a son, and he had been justified in his decision. Nevertheless, as Mrs. Tanaka now pointed out, this had not diminished the nobility of his character, even in describing to her the intensity of his sufferings.

"He did not know," she repeated, "and he chose me, not knowing whether the child would be a boy. In a way he was wrong, for his first duty is to his ancestral family. I cannot say what the new Japanese duty is to his ancestral family. I cannot say what the new Japanese are these days, for we are still an old-fashioned Japanese. My husband believes in his duty. If he had chosen the child, knowing it was a son, I would have said he was right. A son is more important. But he chose me. I owe him everything. So how can I make him unhappy now? I cannot do it. I will not tell him about this wild child. It would be most ungrateful for me to do so."

Elizabeth was dismissed, and she knew it. She rose and put out her hand.

"Thank you, Mrs. Tanaka, for being so frank. Mariko, I shall only ask that you—and your mother—take a little time to think things over again. Perhaps, after our talk—"

Mariko wiped her eyes and put out her hand.

"Thank you—" Her voice was a whisper.

Outside in the sunlit street, Elizabeth sauntered a few blocks and in no haste, her reflective mind considering the human dilemma. A couple passed her, a girl, a boy, hand in hand, and deeply in love, as any eye, however casual, could see. But no eyes were casual. People glanced at them with comprehensive amusement, envy, wistfulness, whatever. This was the way it began—with love. If Tomio loved Mariko, then it was Tomio she must find. And, her mind cleared by resolution, she went back to the office.

When Michelle came in from visiting an adoptive family she was behind her desk as usual.

"So you are here," Michelle said. She took off her coat and sat down, her eyes questions.

"I went to see Mrs. Tanaka," Elizabeth said briskly.

"Did you succeed—"

"I succeeded in nothing but I have not given up."

"Elizabeth, you have told me many times it is better to take the child away when it is not wanted—"

"Well, this time I shall disobey myself," Elizabeth said still more briskly.

"But how—"

"That is my secret," Elizabeth said before the question could be finished.

Her plan was simple. It was to go to the young man and remind him that he was an American, and that as an American he should forget old Japanese customs and acknowledge his child by marrying Mariko at once. And she would do this tonight. In the morning the young man would be at work.

"I shall be working late tonight," she told Michelle now. "Before you go, please put Mariko's file on my desk."

When Michelle laid the file upon her desk and said good night, Elizabeth copied the name and address of Tomio Nagai. He lived, she discovered, in quite a good section of town. There was really no excuse for him, and she decided to be severe. But should she telephone first? No, she would not. He might say that he had an engagement and could not see her. She decided to chance it.

She was not, however, a woman to proceed too quickly. She went to a quiet restaurant and ate a good dinner and lingered over her coffee. It was nine o'clock before the taxi let her out at the address she had written down. The house was old but well kept.

"Which apartment, lady?" the doorman inquired.

"The eighth floor," she said firmly. "Mr. Tomio Nagai."

He looked at her uncertainly, and she remained calm and invincibly respectable.

"Eighth floor, to the right," he said, and let her pass.

The corridor was well carpeted, and on the door to the right was a small brass plate bearing the name Tomio Nagai. She pressed the bell button. A sound of music came from within. Someone was playing the piano very well. She pressed the button again and the music stopped. The door opened and she saw before her a severely handsome young man, unusually tall for a Japanese and with the bearing of a soldier.

"Mr. Tomio Nagai?"

He looked at her with surprise. "Yes."

"I would like to speak with you for a few minutes."

He hesitated. "May I ask—"

"It is about Mariko Tanaka."

For an instant she thought he would shut the door in her face but he did not.

"Come in," he said. "Please sit down."

She entered into a large living room. A small grand piano stood in one corner and sheets of music were scattered on the floor. He stooped to pick them up, arranged them exactly and put them on a shelf in the bookcase. Then he sat down facing her, she on the cherry red couch, he on the matching red chair. Everything else in the room was stone gray with touches of black. There was only one picture, a long landscape scroll in black and white. A young man of taste, this!

There he sat, waiting, distant, wary. She decided to be direct.

"Mr. Nagai, I am Elizabeth Anderson, executive director of a private adoption agency. I am here on behalf of a child. I am sure you know what child. Mariko Tanaka came to our offices yesterday. She asked us to place the child for adoption as soon as it was born."

His handsome dark eyes flickered, but he continued to gaze at her, waiting.

"I think you know whose child it is," she went on.

"She told you?"

"Yes."

He waited so long that she wondered if he were thinking of a way to deny it and she spoke again.

"It is not at all usual for me to speak like this to a young man whose child a young woman wishes to release for adoption. But Mariko Tanaka is not a usual young woman. Nor, as I now see, are you a usual young man. I know something of the circumstances of the family. Without understanding Japanese customs, I can even understand your wish not to wound your father-in-law-to-be. But if you don't become his son you will wound him anyway, won't you?"

Tomio Nagai wet his lips. "I no longer wish to marry."

"Why not?" she inquired.

He gave a great sigh. "It is too complex," he said at last.

"Complex?"

"We could not be happy."

She leaned forward and spoke earnestly. "Mr. Nagai, believe me, this sort of thing happens often—too often, but I have seen it turn out well."

"It does not move me that it happens often," he said coldly. "I know it happens. I was with the American army in Italy. Thank you, Miss Anderson, for your interest. But I have made up my mind."

She was suddenly angry.

"After all," she said as coldly. "It takes two to make a child. You don't mean to imply that you were—seduced? I can scarcely believe that of Mariko."

He looked at her and got up and walked to the piano. He touched the keys softly with his right hand and played a few minor notes of something Japanese. Then he closed the piano and sat down again.

"In a way," he said, "she did seduce me. That is to say—well, it's true that I had—more than once—asked her if she would—you see, in the American army there was a great deal of—let me say, I became quite American. When she and I were first engaged, I was quite—American."

He seemed unable to find the adjective he needed, and compromised merely on "American."

"By that you mean—"

"When men are together without women, and for a long

time," he was hesitating on each word, "the sex act becomes important in one way—in another, not. For me, I would have said—it was—not. I know that many Americans commit the act—perform it, rather—before marriage. Statistics say—"

"Never mind statistics," she said. "They don't seem to apply to you."

He went on as though she had not interrupted.

"But I cannot explain to you why I suddenly became—Japanese. When she yielded to me—I was taken by surprise—totally. As a matter of fact, I—yielded to her!"

"I don't understand."

"Miss Anderson, I will tell you—"

He did tell her, with a frankness so opposite to his first reserve that she could not have believed it except that life had taught her to accept the contradiction. When deep reserve breaks, then there is no reserve. So it was now.

He had begged Mariko several times after they were engaged, he said. He was in constant unease because she resolutely refused him. No, he was not virgin. That was scarcely to be expected of a man passionate by nature. Certainly it was not expected of Japanese men. Nevertheless, he thought of himself as American at that time, and American men, it seemed to him, did not expect even their women to be entirely chaste. In the army, for example, married men, or men only engaged, were constantly depressed when letters were late, because they suspected their wives, or fiancées, of unfaithfulness. In a strange way, he began almost to press Mariko out of jealousy. If she were willing, with him, then he would know her capable of such behavior, with others. In reality he wanted her to refuse him. Yes, certainly, it was cruel, but that was the way he was. And she had always refused him. He began to believe then that she was truly chaste, that she would not receive him into herself until they were married. Yes, it began to be a sort of play between them, he imploring and she refusing, even running away, and he after her. But he never expected—

How had it happened? He could not tell the exact moment when he had changed. It began with the announcement party. His parents were dead—she knew that. Did she know how they had died? Though he was grown and fighting in Italy, he had felt himself orphaned by the news of the tragedy. When he came home there was no one to come to. He had met Mariko at the university where Dr. Tanaka was a professor. He had been invited to the Tanaka home. It began very properly. Dr. Tanaka was a great man and a good one. He was proud when Dr. Tanaka asked him to be his son. Well, yes, he had been reluctant, in a way, to give up the family name, but there were others of the family in Japan, and he was American. The name had not seemed so important as having a family again. And he was proud to be so welcome. Beyond that he had not thought very much. In the army, a man learns not to think. It was only at the announcement party that he really felt deeply what it would mean to be Dr. Tanaka's son because it meant so much to Dr. Tanaka. Everybody had laughed because Dr. Tanaka forgot to announce the engagement, in his excitement to announce his new son.

"I wish to make a happy announcement," he had shouted to the assembled guests. There was champagne and he lifted his glass. "Congratulate me—Tomio Nagai has consented to become my legal son, by marriage!"

The guests had shouted back laughter. "But whom is he to marry?"

Dr. Tanaka had looked about, half-dazed. "True," he said, "I forgot. Where is Mariko? Tomio, find Mariko!"

He had gone in search and found her hiding behind the

curtains in the dining room, and he had led her out. But she had been shy and had only bowed three times to the guests and had run away again.

"Find her—find her!" the guests had shouted, laughing, and so he had gone in search again.

This time it was not so easy. He had not found her at once, not until he had thought of the old, disused carriage house at the end of the long garden. Thither he had gone and he had peered over the board siding of a stall. She was standing there and she did not see him. So he had put his two hands over her head and closed them about her soft throat.

"Shall I choke you," he had asked laughing, "or will you come back where you belong?"

She had laughed back. "Choke me, please—"

He had loosed her then and gone to her side. They had been here before, he and she, and once he had even forced her down to the matted straw, but she had fought him off. Now, strangely, he felt no such desire.

"I want to tell you," he said, and then found it hard to tell her.

She had insisted. "What? Tell me!"

"I love you—I love you more than ever now."

"Why?"

"I don't know. But when your father called me his son, just now—it made me think of my parents. I wish they had not died in that desert."

"Why do you think of them today? It is bad luck to think of death today."

This was what she had said, but he had paid no particular heed to such old superstition. He had simply said he had something to tell her. And he had told her.

"You have been right not to—to—give in to me. I am glad

you have not. I think I would have been ashamed, at this moment—if you had."

Here he paused to gaze anxiously at Elizabeth Anderson.

"Can you understand me thus far?" he inquired.

"Perhaps," she said, "I shall understand better when you have finished. I don't understand yet how it happened after what you have just told me."

"I shall never understand," he said abruptly. He was on his feet again, and he paused before the long scroll. The scene was of mountains rising out of mist. On the gray flank of the mountain a small human figure toiled upward.

He continued. "She had never been willing before to say outright that she loved me. Of course I knew that she did. A man knows. But she wouldn't speak words. She's Japanese, in her own way."

"I love you differently today," he had told her.

"Differently?" she had asked, as though she were frightened.

And suddenly she had flung herself against him. "I love you, I love you," she had cried, "and always the same."

"What do you want?" he had asked roughly.

For she had never pressed against him like that of her own accord, and now when she looked at him, her eyes half-closed, suffused with a sweet weakness, he had simply behaved—call it blindly. He had pressed her backward, holding her as he knelt, until they lay on the matted straw.

It was quickly over. "We've got to get back," he had told her. "They're waiting for us."

So they had arranged their clothing and she brushed the straw out of her hair and they went back to the living room.

"When the guests were gone and the party over," he told Elizabeth Anderson, "I came back here to my own rooms. I was appalled at what I had done. No, it was at what I had allowed to happen. But how could I know that she would suddenly—become so weak? I had trusted to her strength. I wanted her to be strong. Women are supposed to be strong—in such matters—Japanese women—"

He stopped. "I have no right to blame Mariko. But—"

He wheeled on her. "She should have been strong, nevertheless—if she really loved me. She knew very well that I—needed her to be strong—for both of us. That's why the men in Italy felt so—lost. If you can't trust your own woman, then—"

He shrugged and flung out his hands. "That's the story. How can I expect that you will understand?"

Elizabeth considered. What could she say now? She did understand in her own way. The image had been destroyed, the poetic image of the woman, pure and faithful, something of an angel. Only the woman remained—for this man it was not enough, perhaps.

"You still love her?" she inquired.

He shrugged again. "I don't know what you call love. Yes, of course, I love her, as a woman. I'll never get over her. But as a Japanese, I don't want my wife to be the sort that—"

"Ah, but you're American," she said quickly. "You're very American. Just telling me all this—a Japanese couldn't have, could he?"

"I don't know what a Japanese couldn't do," he said almost sullenly. "I only know myself. And I can't go to Dr. Tanaka and say, look I've made your daughter pregnant. He'd not even want me as his son—I've let him down, too—or she has—"

"Can't you two just go off and make an American home together and forget all this family?"

"No," he said flatly. "No, we can't. A branch of a tree can't live by itself. It has to stay on the tree. The tree is the family. We'd stop loving each other, sooner or later, if we just ran away."

"That's Japanese," she retorted.

"Then I'm Japanese," he retorted in turn.

"So what will you do?" she asked.

"Go away alone," he said.

"And Mariko?"

"She'll marry someone else. That's when I'll go back to Japan."

"I can't understand you, after all," she told him.

"I still don't expect you to," he told her.

She rose then. They shook hands and she went away defeated.

The next day dawned clear and mild. Yesterday's storm had sailed out to sea. The air of the city was piercingly clear and Michelle came in as brisk as the morning breeze.

"Do we get the baby?" she asked immediately.

"Not yet," Elizabeth Anderson replied. She came of stubborn blood of Maine ancestors, and she did not yield easily. She had failed with the young man, but she could still go to Dr. Tanaka and see how far she could penetrate his Japanese encasement. Perhaps he was more liberal than they thought. Perhaps his heart would melt at the news of a grandchild, even though but a 'wild' one. She would keep this visit secret, too, even from Michelle.

At ten o'clock, when it could be expected that Dr. Tanaka would be in his office at the university, and one could hope not in class, she made an excuse of a vaguely aching tooth, which was true, for she had a tooth that ached when she was tired or perplexed and she had delayed discovering why.

"I'll be back shortly," she told Michelle.

Shortly she should be, for a few minutes would tell her

whether Dr. Tanaka was the sort of man who could or should be upset by news that was good or bad, depending on how one looked at it. Some men might think it good news to have a grandchild by whatever means.

In less than half an hour she found herself in an office where the sun streamed in and shone upon the gray head of a small kindly man who came out from behind his desk to greet her. He had no secretary and she had simply walked in.

"Dr. Tanaka? I am Elizabeth Anderson."

She put out her hand, deciding instantly at the sight of that friendly wrinkled face not to mention the adoption agency. He would not know what it was!

He looked slightly bewildered, but welcoming.

"Miss Anderson? What can I do for you? Are you one of my students?"

She laughed. "How nice of you! No, I'm not as young as that, I'm afraid."

What reason could she give for being here? Suddenly it seemed impossible to tell the truth, the particular truth, and she seized upon one far less important.

"I've always wanted to visit Japan, Dr. Tanaka. It may be possible for me this next summer. Could you advise me what to see—and do?"

He took the greatest pains to give her advice. He was delighted to take down his books and show her pictures of Kyoto the beautiful, and Mount Fuji, rising out of the clouds, and the other beauties of Japan. And all the time he was showing her himself through his country, his beloved country.

"I wonder you don't go back there, Dr. Tanaka."

He smiled. "America has been too kind to me. I have many friends. In gratitude I have become a citizen. I have two countries—I am rich. But, nevertheless—"

He leaned to whisper to her. "In my will I ask to be

buried in Japan, in the family place. Living, I am American, but my ashes I must return to my ancestors."

It was impossible to tell him, simply impossible. Kind as he was, she did not dare to strike the blow of a second disappointment.

For as he put his books away he prattled on. "And I have great happiness soon in my family. My eldest daughter Mariko—first I must explain that I have no son. Fate has denied me. For a long time I was unhappy—secretly, because I don't wish to make my good wife unhappy, too. Yet without a son, why should I return my ashes to my ancestors? There is no one to take my place in the family when I die. Just another handful of ashes! But now, I will have a son. My daughter will marry soon a fine young man, Tomio Nagai. You know the name? He was given a medal for exceptional bravery in battle. Also he speaks very good Japanese. In fact, he is quite a good Japanese scholar in my classes. I shall recommend him for associate professor as soon as he gets his doctor's degree. American, American born, even, but—well, his parents are dead. They were Japanese. So now I have a son. I have nothing else to ask of life. And I can die in peace. Because I have done my duty to both my countries."

It was indeed impossible to tell him. She could not take the risk. She put out her hand and shook his warmly.

"Thank you, Dr. Tanaka. I hope I can go to Japan."

"I hope so, too," he replied, smiling at her benevolently. "You will understand many things then."

She smiled back, nodded, and was about to take her leave. With her meticulous New England conscience, she stopped by at her dentist's office and made an appointment for the tooth, although it had suddenly stopped aching. Then she went back to the office.

"Why are you in such dark study?" Michelle inquired in the course of the afternoon.

"Brown is the color, I believe," she replied. "I am in a brown study, because we must somehow help Mrs. Tanaka, and I don't know how. Perhaps no one can help her. Perhaps she has to do it herself."

"Mrs. Tanaka?" Michelle repeated blankly.

"Yes. She's quite right. The baby doesn't belong in that family. I see that, though I can't understand it, not being Japanese myself. In all innocence, that baby would destroy the family. Don't ask why just now, Michelle. It's much too long a story—too involved. But we must take the baby and then Tomio Nagai must marry Mariko whether he wants to or not. And the three of them, they and Mrs. Tanaka, must keep the secret of the baby for the rest of their lives. I love truth but it can't be told. Now please go away. I have a telephone call to make. And you can choose the best young couple we have waiting—talk it over with me later."

When the door was closed, she made the call. It was long and it was to Mrs. Tanaka.

"Mrs. Tanaka? Are you alone? Then I must confess to you—I went to see Dr. Tanaka today . . . No, no, I told him nothing. You are entirely right. He must not be told. But, as you said, the marriage must take place. You must tell Mariko she has to marry Tomio if I take the baby. Absolutely."

She waited while Mrs. Tanaka made cries of surprise and then of pleasure. Then she went on.

"I have something more to confess. I went to see Tomio . . . last night. . . . But he does want to belong to your family. . . . He very much wants to be Dr. Tanaka's son! . . . But he has to understand that it is his *duty* to be Dr. Tanaka's son. His Japanese duty. Else Dr. Tanaka will have lost everything."

"Everything?" Mrs. Tanaka repeated.

"I mean, his beautiful sacrifice, the one he made to save your life—will be just useless, don't you see? He really deserves a son, don't you think? And you can give a son to him. Tomio and Mariko have no right to ruin his life—and make it impossible for him to be buried in Japan."

Mrs. Tanaka gasped. "How you know everything!"

"So, Mrs. Tanaka," she went on crisply, "you and Mariko and Tomio must sacrifice yourselves for Dr. Tanaka's sake. You will make the two young people see that. But I think it won't be a sacrifice."

She paused, aghast at what she had said. She turned her head away and murmured to herself, "My god, what am I saying—the baby is the sacrificial lamb!"

"What are you saying, please?" Mrs. Tanaka inquired. "I can't quite hear you."

She returned to the telephone. "I am saying that I will find the very best home for the baby, wonderful young parents, longing for a child and unable to have one by birth. So don't worry about the baby. That's where I come in. I have a duty, too. I understand that much, anyway."

There was a long silence at the other end of the telephone. She heard Mrs. Tanaka's voice at last.

"Thank you," the voice said. "Thank you very much. Forever!"

Dream Child

AMERICA, KOREA—1960S

IT WAS THE END of another day. He had not noticed the in-
creasing dusk until the telephone on his desk rang. He took
up the receiver.

"Martin Baynes speaking—"

A light voice, a gay voice, fluttered at his ear. "Oh, I don't
want to bother you, Martin—just your secretary."

He laughed. Something about this voice of hers always
made him laugh. Or else it was simply that his heart lifted
whenever she called. "She's gone, Faye. It must be past five
o'clock."

"Then why are you still there?"

"I'm trying to make up my mind about something."

"Business?"

"No."

She waited but he did not proceed and he could imagine
the shrug of her pretty shoulders.

"Meaning you won't tell me?"

"Meaning—I don't know what."

"Now you're teasing me."

"Really I'm not. Anything I can do for you?"

She hesitated and then hurried on. "What I wanted to ask
Miss Bates was—do you have anything on for tonight? If you
had, I'd just—not mention it."

"I haven't and what's *it?*"

"I have tickets for *Madame Butterfly*. Mother's got a cold
and Dad won't go without her."

"*Madame Butterfly!* That's pretty old stuff for you, isn't it?"

"You're insulting me, aren't you? It's opera."

"Not pop!"

"I'd like to go, for once—I can't tell you why. Maybe because you were over there."

"Not Japan, my child—Korea."

"It's over there, just the same. Shall we?"

"Of course. Have dinner with me. I'll pick you up at six-thirty."

"Oh good! Thank you, Martin."

Her voice sang in his ear and he smiled as he put up the receiver. She was so much younger than he that sometimes he wondered if the difference was too great, her twenty years to his thirty. But years were not the real difference. She had lived in the shelter of that great house and he had been on his own since he left the orphanage when he was sixteen. He had never known his parents. They had produced him somewhere, somehow, and he had been found on the steps of a church on a Sunday morning. He was, he had been told, not more than ten days or two weeks old. The minister, stumbling over the basket which contained him, had picked him up, basket and all, and had taken him to the orphanage. But her father, Roger Walters, had given him his first job. He had been errand boy, janitor, and man of all work in the store, a hardware business in this suburb of Philadelphia. Now, years later of course, he was the junior partner. Roger Walters, lacking a son, had treated him kindly and except for the two years in South Korea he had spent his life here. Someday, he supposed, he would—

The telephone rang again, as he was straightening his desk. He took up the receiver.

"Yes?"

It was Faye once more. "Martin, I'm bothering you but I forgot to tell you—it's dinner jacket for you, Mother says."

"Oh, all right. Thanks for letting me know."

"And, Martin—"

"Yes, Faye?"

"Shall I wear a red dress or a white one?"

He laughed. "Must I decide?"

"Of course you must. You'll be looking at it all evening."

"Looking at you, not the dress! All right—the white one."

"Oh—"

"You'd rather wear the red?"

"I think the zipper is broken on the white one."

She made him laugh again. "Oh, come now, Faye—you're teasing me."

"Truly it is broken! Well, we'll see—white or red. I'll meet you in an hour, Martin."

She hung up and he left his office, smiling. That was the joy of her, the eternal, changing, diverting, teasing mischief in her. He was a solemn chap, he knew, a man who took life too seriously. But his life had been too serious, and now with the boy continually on his mind, his son, let him never forget, whom he had not been able to explain to Faye, and yet whom he must explain before he could in honor ask her to marry him, although how could he explain to her that which he could scarcely understand in himself?

Walking briskly down the street to his own small house, where he lived alone, he felt the old vague agony sweep over him like a dark cloud over the sky. The unutterable loneliness of his life had overwhelmed him time and again, and in its recurring shadow he had, four years ago, returned to Korea for a month's vacation. It had become necessary to him to relive that part of his life, to find, if he could, a girl whom he could not entirely forget. He had met her only a week before he had been discharged from the service, but in that week she had made herself indispensable to him, so that parting from her had been surprisingly difficult.

When he returned to Korea, however, he had found no trace of the girl he remembered. Instead there had been another girl, Minyi, a pretty creature with whom he spent six days. When he came home again he began to fall in love with Faye, at first because there was something alike in the two women, Faye and the girl he could not find, so distant in time and space and yet alike in a certain warm gaiety, a mingling of child and woman, a quality he needed to keep away his private agony, inexplicable but the result, he supposed, of his barren childhood and the sense of belonging to no one and having no one to belong to him.

Of the brief days spent with Minyi, to his chagrin, a child had been born, a son, whom of course he had never seen. But she had sent photographs over the years and he could imagine a look of himself in the little boy, now more than three years old. It was difficult for him to comprehend his own feelings about this child. Here surely was something, someone, of his own, and he felt a certain rueful pride in having a son, however inconveniently, and he had even named him Marty, an abbreviation of his own name. Yet how could he tell Faye? Impossible to tell her, equally impossible not to! His troubled mind reviewed often every moment of the time he had spent with Minyi. He did not love her, could never love her, and yet as the mother of his child, he was somehow related to her, and in decency he must rid himself of this relation before he could ask Faye to marry him.

The old agony fell upon him very heavily indeed as he entered his house and closed the door behind him and locked it, as though he feared someone might come in, as though even Minyi. Yet she had entered in her own way, writing him begging letters, telling him how she needed money for the boy's new shoes, a bigger coat, for food and the rent money for the shack where she still lived. There was a letter from her at this very moment, as he saw. It was lying on the hall table where the maid put the mail every day. The letter was on top, the Korean airmail stamp—well, he had better get it over with. He tore the envelope open and a photograph fell out. It was of the boy alone, the first picture she had sent of him without her. He stared at it, forgetful of everything. A fine-looking boy, healthy and apparently happy! He'd sent vitamins regularly, remembering his own hungry childhood in the poor orphanage, and he had ordered Minyi to see that the child had plenty of meat.

He glanced over the letter now, her usual begging letter, he saw at once. But no, she had added a sentence.

"Some day you come here taking him Stateside, so I talk him good English for you."

Bring the child here? He had thought of it, not Minyi, of course but only the child, whom perhaps he and Faye could adopt as though he were a stray orphan, as in effect he was, having no real father, that is to say, a day-to-day father in the house with him, teaching him, loving him. The letter drifted to the floor and he was gazing at the boy's picture again. Of course he must go and fetch the boy. Faye would love him, surely, and if she did not—well, he owed a debt to the child. His own parents had deserted him to strangers and he must not desert his son. True, the child had a mother, but what could Minyi do for a child whose father was American? Nothing—nothing at all! No, he must not desert his son. He made the decision. Suddenly the agony left him and he dashed up the stairs to dress.

"You're different this evening," Faye said.

"Because you're wearing the white dress," he replied, smiling. "It's a triumph for a man, isn't it?"

"You knew I'd wear it," she said softly, her eyes teasing him, tempting.

They were at the dinner table, and he felt nearer to her than ever before. Yes, he was in love with her. Yes, he would ask her to marry him as soon as—as soon as—

"We'll be late," she exclaimed. "We'll miss the first act!"

There was no time to tell her now, no time to explain, no time for talk of marriage, certainly. They arrived at the theater in a whirl of gaiety, running up the steps hand in hand. She threw her white mink evening coat to the attendant at the checking room while he stood impatiently at the ticket window. They barely reached the doors before they were closed and, tiptoeing up the aisle as the music began, they found their seats, fortunately at the end of a row. Then irresistibly he found himself drawn into the opera. He had never heard it before and as the story unfolded, he felt a return of the old agony. If Minyi had been like Madame Butterfly— but she was not and had never been. Madame Butterfly was a beautiful woman, and Minyi had been—was—merely a pretty little slant-eyed girl, too untaught to find a job, too poor to survive without one—or without a man, preferably an American, because Americans had money. No, let him be just! At least she had taken care of the boy, she had been a good mother. He owed her much. Agonizing, the darkness of the shadow upon him again, he saw himself as the lieutenant in the opera, leaving a lover, a child, behind him in a strange country. For of course the country would be strange to the child, too, though he was born there, for the child himself was a stranger, belonging to no country. This was the real tragedy of Madame Butterfly, that she had given birth to a child who was a stranger in the land of his birth, unless his father claimed him. And he, he himself, Martin Baynes, was that father.

The opera drew to its close. He saw Faye wiping her eyes and he reached for her hand and heard her murmuring voice. "How *could* he—I *hate* him! The poor little child!"

He was about to come to the man's defense and then could not, for it would have been to defend himself. He released her hand abruptly, under the pretense of helping her with her coat.

Outside in the brisk night air of early spring they continued in silence. Even in the car as he was driving her home, speech was difficult.

"It's made us sad," she said at last.

"Yes," he said, "because it is sad."

And he made up his mind yet again. No, he would not tell her. The burden was his and he must rid himself of guilt before he told her. He must go back once more to Korea, find his son and bring him home. Then and then only could he ask Faye to marry him.

Two weeks later he was in Korea and walking down the narrow lane he remembered so well. Here among other small houses was the one where his son lived. How should he meet this child who was his son? He would open his arms to him. He would behave as so often he had imagined, when he himself was a child, that his own father would behave. But his father had never come in search of the child he had begotten. His own father had never even left him a name. Baynes had been the name the orphanage had given him. At least his own child would have a name. He would go to the American Embassy and declare his paternity. Then, if Minyi would give up the child, he would take him home and together they would appear before Faye and she would see the whole story, for of course the boy would look enough like the father to declare himself without words. That was another question. Had Minyi taught him English—enough, that is, to carry on a conversation? Minyi had a patois of her own, gathered from American men she had known. He had never asked Minyi about those men. Simply, in excess of loneliness, lonely by birth and especially in this lonely foreign land, he had lived in her small house for six days, drinking, he must confess, and sleeping with her. What had got into him? He had not drunk to excess before or since. Yet for six days he had been another man, a different being, as though he had slipped into another skin. And Minyi had been warm and willing and not more venal than others, he was sure.

He recognized her house at this moment, a square of mud brick wedged in between others. The spring wind fluttered ragged garments hanging on a pole outside the door. Would she be at home in the middle of the day like this? Sleeping, likely! Sleeping she was when he stepped into the door. It hung half open and he gave it a push and looked in and there she lay on the board bed, wrapped in an old quilt, her short black hair a tousle on a small flat pillow.

"Minyi," he said gently.

She did not hear and he went to her and shook her by the shoulder but still gently. She woke then, and turned over and stared at him, her face blank. She had aged, he saw at once. The girlish roundness was gone from her face, and her high cheekbones stood out in angles.

"Minyi," he said again.

She sat up and pushed back her hair.

"Why you come?" she demanded.

He sat down on a wooden stool. "I've come to see the boy."

"Boy?" she repeated.

"My boy," he repeated. "You know—Marty, my son."

"Oh-h-h, yaas—"

She gave him a quick look and then climbed down from

the bed and thrust her bare feet into leather shoes, high-heeled ones, he observed, but now worn down and shapeless.

"Where is he?"

"He?"

"Marty," he said impatiently now. "Wake up, Minyi! I've come a long way to see him."

She sat down by a low table and felt of the teapot. "Cold," she muttered. "I fix you hot."

"Never mind about tea! Where is Marty?"

She looked at him quickly and then turned her head. "Too bad you are coming. He dead now."

"Dead?" He stared at her unbelieving. "When did he die?"

She counted on her fingers. "Nine—ten days. Very quick. In morning fine, he get up eat, go out for play. Night he hot, crying alla time, die very quick."

"Did you get the doctor?"

"No doctor here. Anyway, I no got money, see?"

"But I've sent you money!"

"Yaas—you send, but he eat too much, very big size, alla time new clothes—something."

"And you sit there," he blurted. "You haven't a tear in your eyes!"

She shrugged, not comprehending, and lit a small spirit lamp to heat water for tea. He was seized with sudden terrible anger.

"Minyi, look here!"

She looked at him, her shallow, still pretty face almost sullen. He shouted at her.

"I don't believe you, see? I don't believe he is dead! You've hidden him!"

She was angry in turn. "Why I hide? You talk silly. I not hide. He dead, I tell you."

He hunched his shoulders, trying not to weep, trying to

think sensibly about the impossible. His little boy, his son, dead! He lifted his head suddenly.

"Where are his clothes?"

She was putting tea leaves into a small earthen teapot. "Cloes?"

"Yes! The red sweater I sent you before Christmas—the slacks and socks—everything!"

"Oh yass—I give away his frien'—very nice boy—poor mother like me, American GI father go Stateside—he no send money—"

She was pouring the boiling water over the tea leaves and she held the pot in her hands to warm them.

"Haven't you anything here of his?" he demanded.

"What thing?" she replied.

She was well awake now and suddenly she smiled at him, a smile unexpectedly sweet, even pretty. It was the smile that first attracted him, but at this moment it sickened him. He remembered suddenly the words that had followed the smile. To his amazement she spoke them again now.

"You so nice man!"

"Oh, shut up," he muttered under his breath.

"You sorry now—never mind. I make baby for you again —no sweat."

He got up. "No, thanks!" he said.

And was leaving her forever except that at the door he was constrained to pause and try once more. After all, a child was a living creature. Marty could not be completely gone as though he had never existed. He sat down again.

"Minyi, who was with you when he died?"

"He die sleep." She glanced at him and as though the misery of his eyes compelled her, she wiped her eyes on the end of the bow that tied her short jacket over her bosom.

"Did no one see him dead?"

"My girl friend, he see."

"Where is your girl friend?"

"He got business now with American GI."

"Where is the grave?"

"No grave—just take away."

"Minyi, how could you—" he broke off, his lip trembling. Suddenly he turned and dashed out of the miserable house. As directly as a homing bird he went to the hotel and locking himself in his room he threw himself on the bed and sobbed. His son—his little son, living alone, dying alone! For what sort of a mother had he been given? And given by whom but himself, the father? He hated himself, vile human being that he was to copulate with a stranger and out of that wild and lawless act to create a son. He was no whit better than his own father who begat him as carelessly as he had begotten Marty. Then, his tears spent, he got up and washed his face and brushed his hair and sat down to think. Perhaps Minyi was still lying. Perhaps her girl friend would tell him the truth. Next morning, tomorrow morning, he would go early enough to find her still asleep—no use going now for she would indeed be at her "business"—and force the truth from her.

He spent the day in restless walking the streets, then went to bed and could not sleep.

He woke early and in the gray morning light he knew he must try once again, try only once more, before he left this foreign country never to return. He must talk to someone else before his final attack upon Minyi—someone else who had seen Marty when he was a baby, a toddler, a little boy, someone else who had seen him dead. Then he could go home, certain at least of death. For to what deception could Minyi not have fallen? She might have left the child somewhere, with someone, a relative perhaps, so that she would be more free to pursue her own lost ways. Truth—truth from a witness was what he must have, and certainty, even of death.

He rose and showered and dressed and went downstairs so early that the waiters, setting the tables in the hotel dining room, stared at him reproachfully. He sat down at a table near the door.

"Breakfast!" he ordered.

"No can," a waiter said promptly.

"Yes, can," he insisted. "Anyway, toast and coffee."

In the end he had bacon and eggs and thus reinforced he felt determination strengthen his will. Absolutely he would not leave this country without finding Marty or knowing why he was not to be found.

In the morning still gray, he took a cab, a small black affair made of beer cans hammered around a jeep engine, probably stolen, and arrived at what seemed to be predawn in the lane he had visited yesterday. Obviously the women were all asleep after the night's work. A few children played here and there, however, and he looked at them with a catch in his heart. They were all older than Marty would have been. No —wait, there beside Minyi's door played a small boy in a red sweater, the very sweater he had sent Marty last Christmas. He was three or four years old—a big three, but then the half-American children were always bigger than the others. He went nearer and stood watching the child. Yes—yes—it might be Marty. He walked toward him, not too fast, and stood looking down on the top of his tousled dark head. The little fellow was making something out of mud. A ball? No, a toy man.

"Marty," he said under his breath. Only why would Minyi lie to him?

The child did not lift his head or look up but went on industriously, shaping the stubby figure.

"Is it you, Marty?" he asked.

Still there was no answer. Then he stooped and looked into the child's face.

"Yes—it's you—or could be!"

He put his hand under the child's chin and lifted it so that he could see the face. Of course he knew the face. It was the one he had seen in the photographs, the one he had watched change from a baby to a boy. Wait until he found Minyi and told her he knew she was lying! He released the child and stood up. At this moment a door opened into the shack next to Minyi's and a strong, stout young woman came out. She seized the little boy by the arm and slapped his cheek.

"Bad boy!" she cried. Then she smiled at Martin. "He too bad—alla time play in mud."

"Where is his mother?" he demanded.

The woman tapped her breast. "Me his mother."

"You?"

"Yeah. His father American—he go Stateside."

"Minyi is not his mother?"

The woman laughed. "Minyi no gotta boy. She never gotta baby."

"But that sweater—"

"Yeah, I buy sweater from her for my boy. Minyi no gotta boy, I say."

"I sent money—"

"You? You her boyfriend?"

The woman looked half frightened for an instant and then her rough face broke and she laughed loudly. "You come back? Now Minyi got trouble, I think! She take my boy for picture to you. She say never you come back. Never mind—be sorry for her! She too poor—alla time sick, no money, no catch GI. GI like healthy girl. So—you come! No-no, this my boy. Minyi give me twenty *won* take many picture for you. Yeah—too bad—she gotta no baby for you—never!"

He stood staring, listening, bewildered. Marty had not even been born! He was only a dream child. Yet whose fault was it that he had been a dream? Still his own—still his own! He would have to tell Faye about him, though he had never existed. For to all intents he had existed. So far as he himself was concerned, he had made it possible for Marty to be born. It was only Minyi's imperfect body that had not completed the creation.

He turned away abruptly, his heart in a turmoil. He was grateful, he was sad. He felt shaken, whether by relief or joy, or by disappointment, it was impossible to tell. Only one thing was clear. He must get home. He must go to Faye and tell her everything—everything! And then as he turned to escape, he heard the woman's voice shouting after him.

"You wanta boy you take this boy—take him Stateside for you! Fifty dollar—you take him!"

He did not reply.

"Queer thing," he said to Faye. "I remember the boy's eyes were blue—Asian eyes, but blue. I wonder if—"

He broke off and smiled but painfully, for she had listened to his story almost in silence. He had blurted it all out this first evening, and of necessity, for all the way home on the jet, or in hotel rooms, he had rehearsed what he would say, until it burned in his brain. Now he had said it. They were sitting in their favorite restaurant, a small Chinese place where none of their friends or family ever came. Here at their habitual table in a corner by a window he had ordered their usual dishes and then had told her abruptly, baldly, hiding nothing, excusing no one, least of all himself. She had listened in silence, asking no questions, her brown eyes fixed on his face. Did she understand, could she understand, how a lonely and bewildered human being, a man, could seize a brief companionship, even with a stranger? Could she understand how it was that he felt now a strange loss, as though the child who had never been born seemed instead to be one who had died?

"You wonder what?" she now inquired when he paused.

"Whether if my—my own son would have had blue eyes like his."

"Likely," she said. "You have the bluest eyes I've ever seen in a human face. All your children will have blue eyes."

"My children," he repeated stupidly.

"Ours," she amended.

Comprehending suddenly, he put out his hand for hers across the table.

"Faye—do you mean—you will—marry me?"

"Of course," she said calmly, her small hand firm in his grasp. "Of course because I understand how it happened. Do you think I could fail to understand anything about you? Only—"

"Only what?"

"That little boy playing in the mud—"

"Yes?"

"Do you think we should leave him there in the mud? So far away?"

He was bewildered. What a confusion of children! Her brown eyes were dancing and sparkling. Was she teasing him? No, not teasing! Suddenly her eyes were grave. "I mean—with a woman who doesn't want him."

"She's his mother, Faye."

"Only by chance," she told him. "And only of his body, Martin. She doesn't love her blue-eyed child so he doesn't belong there, Martin. We must bring him home. On our honeymoon we'll go and fetch him and bring him home."

He gazed at her intensely, absorbing her meaning. Incomprehensible woman! Pragmatic female! She had simply put aside all he had told her as something past and therefore finished. It was of no interest to her. Instead her practical mind laid its hold upon the one important and present fact. There was a blue-eyed child in the wrong country. Never mind whose child he was. He existed, homeless and alien where he was born, and he must find a home. That was her decision, as a woman. That was her instinctive concern.

He gave a great sigh of relief and comprehension. She had suddenly put everything into proportion for him. The load slipped away. What was past was ended and Marty, the child who never was, was lost forever in the shadows of nonexistence. In his place he saw another child stepping into the light of here and now, and following that child others, his own.

"Of course I've always meant to marry you," she said now.

He laughed in relief. "Thanks," he said. "I'd suspected, and I'm glad."

Footsteps padded across the floor. The old Chinese restaurant keeper set a big bowl on the table.

"Bean curd soup," he announced. "You like very much?"

"Great," Martin said. "We do like very much—everything."